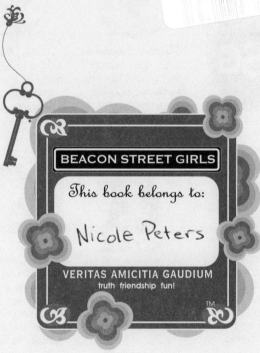

BEACON STREET GIRLS

This book belongs to:

Nicole Peters

VERITAS AMICITIA GAUDIUM
truth friendship fun!

™

Who's Who

BSG

Katani Summers
a.k.a. Kgirl ... Katani has a strong fashion sense and business savvy. She is stylish, loyal & cool.

Avery Madden
Avery is passionate about all sports and animal rights. She is energetic, optimistic & outspoken.

Charlotte Ramsey
A self-acknowledged "klutz" and an aspiring writer, Charlotte is all too familiar with being the new kid in town. She is intelligent, worldly & curious.

Isabel Martinez
Her ambition is to be an artist. She was the last to join the Beacon Street Girls. She is artistic, sensitive & kind.

Maeve Kaplan-Taylor
Maeve wants to be a movie star. Bubbly and upbeat, she wears her heart on her sleeve. She is entertaining, friendly & fun.

Ms. Razzberry Pink
The stylishly pink proprietor of the "Think Pink" boutique is chic, gracious & charming.

Marty
The adopted best dog friend of the Beacon Street Girls is feisty, cuddly & suave.

Happy Lucky Thingy and alter ego Mad Nasty Thingy
Marty's favorite chew toy, it is known to reveal its alter ego when shaken too roughly. He is most often happy.

more on beaconstreetgirls.com

Be sure to read all of our books:

BSG Special Adventure Books:

Coming soon:

ALADDIN MIX

Simon & Schuster Children's Publishing Division

1230 Avenue of the Americas, New York, NY 10020

Copyright © 2004 by B*tween Productions, Inc.,

Home of the Beacon Street Girls

Beacon Street Girls, Kgirl, B*tween Productions, B*Street, and the characters Maeve, Avery, Charlotte, Isabel, Katani, Marty, Nick, Anna, Joline, and Happy Lucky Thingy are registered trademarks and/or copyrights of B*tween Productions, Inc.

All rights reserved, including the right of reproduction in whole or in part in any form.

ALADDIN PAPERBACKS, ALADDIN MIX, and related logo are

registered trademarks of Simon & Schuster, Inc.

Designed by Dina Barsky

The text of this book was set in Palatino Linotype.

Manufactured in the United States of America

First Aladdin Paperbacks edition May 2008

8 10 9 7

Library of Congress Control Number 2008920650

ISBN-13: 978-1-4169-6426-1

ISBN-10: 1-4169-6426-6

1109 FFG

BEACON STREET GIRLS

Letters from the Heart

BY
ANNIE BRYANT

ALADDIN MIX

NEW YORK   LONDON   TORONTO   SYDNEY

ೞ

Letters from
the Heart

Part One
Breaking Apart

open with care!

LOVE

Letters from the Heart

FRAGILE

The Sox Rock!

There wasn't a single seat left on the crowded trolley pulling away from the Fenway T station, but the five Beacon Street Girls couldn't care less.

"Hang on!" Maeve cried, grabbing Isabel's arm as the train lurched, gathering speed as it rolled along the tracks toward Longwood.

It was late afternoon on Sunday, and all the girls— Maeve, Katani, Avery, Charlotte, and their newest friend, Isabel—were coming back from a late-season baseball game. The Red Sox had gotten trounced, but that didn't squelch the girls' spirits. Not one bit.

"Next year's the year," Avery declared, pointing to the big Red Sox logo on her navy blue sweatshirt. Everyone laughed. The legend in Boston was always that *next year* the Sox would do it. And in the meantime, it was fun just being loyal fans. Especially this afternoon. Maeve's father had given her five free tickets, and she'd been able to treat all of her friends to the game.

"How did your dad get those tickets again?" Avery asked.

"My dad showed a movie about the Red Sox at the Movie House," Maeve shrugged. "I'm not sure why, but one of the public relations people for the team gave him a bunch of tickets."

"Lucky," Avery sighed. "I wish my mom had a cool job like your dad does, Maeve. It must be amazing running a movie house."

Maeve couldn't help but agree. But it was funny to see Avery getting so excited about it now—all because of free baseball tickets! Avery's interest in movies tended to run to sports spectaculars anyway.

"Yeah," Isabel was saying, looking a little sad. "You have the perfect family, Maeve." Isabel missed her family being together. Her dad was still back in Detroit, and she, her sister, and her mom were living now in Brookline with her Aunt Lourdes.

Charlotte nodded enthusiastically. "Your dad is SO nice. And he and your mom get to work together ... that's pretty cool."

The trolley turned another corner, and everyone shrieked, trying to hang on to the poles or to each other.

"Yeah, my mom doesn't like to take anything free from anyone," Katani said. "When you're a lawyer, you never know when somebody might be related to a client or something. So my dad doesn't take anything either because he's married to my mom. They both love their jobs so they say they don't care." She shook her head. "Personally, I think you are totally lucky, Maeve. I mean, everybody always wants Red Sox tickets."

The perfect family, Maeve thought. Was that true? She'd never really thought about it that way before. There were just the four of them—herself, her mom, dad, and her little brother, Sam.

The thought of "Sam" and "perfect" in the same sentence cracked Maeve up. "I think you're forgetting something," she reminded her friends. "Remember the Brainiac? The guy whose idea of humor is bringing your underwear out into the living room when your friends come over? The guy who puts toothpaste in your slippers and claims it's an EXPERIMENT?" She pretended to shudder. "I don't think Sam exactly rates as perfect, you guys. Hate to burst your bubble ..."

"Well, but your parents," Isabel persisted. "Your mom and dad are totally perfect together. It's so awesome the way she helps him in the Movie House."

Maeve thought about that. Maybe Isabel was right. She'd never thought about her parents as being perfect for each other ... funny, the way you tend to take that stuff for granted.

The conversation shifted back to the Red Sox, and soon all five girls were chattering away about the game again. But Isabel's words kept ringing in Maeve's ears.

The perfect family. Maeve had the perfect family.

CHAPTER

1

Making History

Ms. O'Reilly faced her seventh-grade social studies class, arms crossed and a quizzical smile on her face. She had written a question in big capital letters on the blackboard and was looking expectantly at her students.

"Can anyone answer this?" she asked, gesturing with a piece of chalk at the board.

Maeve, her laptop open on her desk, typed out the question. It helped her to organize her notes this way, but Ms. O'Reilly's question looked just as puzzling blinking out at her on her laptop screen. Maeve pushed back her long red curls, reading it one more time.

"WHAT IS HISTORY?"

Dillon Johnson's hand shot up. "I can answer that," he said. Leave it to Dillon to be the first to respond. Filled with self-confidence, he was one of the most popular guys in seventh grade at Abigail Adams Junior High. Blond, handsome Dillon was often the first with his hand up. Maeve snapped to attention—she'd had a secret crush on Dillon for awhile now.

Maeve popped open a new window on her laptop. Thank

❂ 4 ❂

the stars for spell check, she thought. Maeve's dyslexia was a continuing source of frustration, and computers gave her the extra support she needed. Of course, Anna and Joline, alias *Queens of Mean*, rolled their eyes every time she opened it up. But for the most part, the laptop was just part of everyday life, and Maeve had almost forgotten that there was anything special about it.

....

Note to Self:
I don't know much about Dillon and
history ... but I'd sure like to be part
of his future. Love the blue eyes.

She had a brief, sudden vision: Future History. Sitting with Dillon ... at the Academy Awards. Maeve in a daring pink evening dress, the sort of color redheads NEVER wear, unless they were superconfident fashion pioneers like Maeve. She pictured Dillon sitting beside her in a tuxedo, looking incredible, just a little older and more sophisticated. *And the award for this year's best actress goes to ... Maeve Kaplan-Taylor!*

Why not? A girl can dream, can't she?

OK—maybe not in the middle of social studies. Maeve dragged her attention back to the blackboard. And to Dillon.

"History," Dillon said, clearing his throat and not sounding so certain he knew the answer anymore, "is—uh, well—you know—stuff that happened before. You know—in the past."

Pete Wexler, one of Dillon's best friends and the quarterback on the J.V. football team, gave him a high-five. A couple of kids laughed.

Betsy Fitzgerald raised her hand, sneaking a glance at

Dillon. Betsy *always* had the right answer. Perfect grades, perfect papers, perfect scores on every test—but unfortunately, a lot of attitude about always being right, too. Whenever Betsy got anything less than 100 percent, she begged and pleaded to get her grade changed. Dillon joked that she was a Type A+.

"History is the study of important events in the past," she said, with a kind of "Aha!" sound in her voice that made Dillon glare at her. Maeve thought Betsy sounded like a newscaster— or like she was repeating something that she'd read in a book.

"That's what I said," Dillon muttered.

Ms. O'Reilly lifted up her chalk. "Okay. Tell me this," she said, her voice suggesting that a challenge was coming. "Everyone watch. Dillon—catch!" She tossed the chalk to Dillon, who caught it in one smooth motion.

Pete Wexler whistled approvingly. "Nice catch," he exclaimed.

Anna and Joline tipped their heads closer together to whisper something to each other. The rest of the class erupted in laughter and conversation, but Maeve was still busy admiring Dillon. Wow! When did he get those muscles? Nice catch was right! She smiled at Pete's unintended pun.

♡ ....

Note to Self:
D.J. is definitely the HOTTEST guy in the whole grade.

She inspected her sentence and added a little smiley icon to finish it off. *Perfect.*

"Now," Ms. O'Reilly continued, pacing back and forth in front of the classroom. "Did that count as history? Throwing that piece of chalk?"

"Of course not," Betsy said, smoothing back her dark hair. "It wasn't important enough. History is about *important* events—like wars. And presidential elections."

Ms. O'Reilly's eyes sparkled. Young and dynamic, with a stylish crop of auburn curls and a round, enthusiastic face, she was one of the most challenging and well-liked teachers in the seventh grade. She really made her students think, and she never let a discussion shut down with an easy or expected answer. "Is it?" she demanded, her green eyes moving from one student to the next. "Is history only the record of the big events, or is it also the story of individual lives and experiences?"

Isabel Martinez raised her hand, looking slightly tentative. Maeve leaned forward to listen. Isabel, who had moved to Boston last month, had already become one of her closest friends. Along with Avery, Katani, and Charlotte, they were the Beacon Street Girls—the name they'd given themselves—a name that had stuck. The five of them had already been through more challenges, adventures, and good times than Maeve could count.

"I'm not sure," Isabel began slowly, "but I think history is also what happens to regular people. My grandfather loves telling my sister and me about what Mexico was like when he was little. And that seems kind of like history to me, too."

Ms. O'Reilly's eyes lit up. "Thank you, Isabel," she said warmly. "I think you're absolutely right. History is NOT just about presidents and wars, but also about individuals. About their experiences, their challenges and struggles, and their stories. For the next three weeks, our class is going to be learning about history from a special perspective. By way of introducing our unit on immigration in the twentieth century, we're going to be creating a classroom museum based upon our collective experiences. We'll call it the Heritage Museum, and it will remain on display for the rest of the grading period."

Ms. O'Reilly proceeded to tell the class a little about her own family's history. "My family came to America from Ireland in the 1890s and settled in South Boston," she explained. Maeve tried to imagine Ms. O'Reilly with a family. She pictured a smaller version of her teacher, every bit as round-faced and smiley as she was today, holding her mother's hand. She had to keep herself from laughing out loud.

....

Note to Self:
Teachers as kids ... very strange thought.

She ran down the list of her teachers in her mind. Mr. Sherman taught pre-algebra. It was impossible to picture him one minute younger. Mr. Maxwell, the computer teacher ... well, he was only in his twenties. Maeve could easily see him younger. Geeky, to be exact. Madame Dupin, her French teacher ... well, she was not so sure about that. Madame Dupin was nice enough, but a little too grandmotherly with her gray hair and comfortable shoes to imagine her much younger. Of course, there was the infamous day Henry Yurt, mispronouncing Madame, called her, Madummy Dupin instead of Madame Dupin, and the class went totally crazy with laughter. On that day, Madame Dupin's pale blue eyes did look kind of mischievous. OK, so maybe she was kind of fun when she was a girl. But Mr. McCarthy, the P.E. teacher—no way could Maeve picture him any age other than forty-three. Not to mention a cranky forty-three. Maeve didn't like him. He played favorites—he really only liked the jocks—and Maeve definitely wasn't a jock.

But what was she doing? There was no time now to keep imagining younger versions of her teachers. Maeve turned her attention back to Ms. O'Reilly, who was walking over to her desk and opening up a big cardboard box.

She took out a heavy glass, ornately carved. "My great-grandfather was a glassmaker. This is one of the glasses that he made when he worked in a factory in Ireland." Then she held up a framed map. "This is a map of Waterford county in Ireland where my family came from. Waterford crystal is some of the most famous crystal in the world. And this ..." She paused as she held up a small piece of paper. "This is a ticket from a ship leaving Ireland and going to Boston in 1849. It belonged to someone in my mother's family—we are not sure whose ticket it was. But we do know, because of the date, that he or she must have left Ireland at the height of the Irish Famine."

"What kind of famine?" asked Katani in a concerned voice.

"It was caused by a blight that damaged most of the potato crop in Ireland for years, and British land policies that forced Irish farmers who couldn't pay their rent off their farms. Close to a million Irish died from hunger and disease. And many more immigrated to America. They came here sick and tired but determined to have better lives."

The class was silent for a moment—many of them imagining what it must have been like for these brave people to come to America so long ago.

"Now, what I'm going to ask you to do over the next few weeks is to create your own display in our class's collective Heritage Museum. To begin, each one of you is going to do some research into your own family's history. Have you always lived in the same place? Where did your parents come from, or your grandparents, or great-grandparents? How did they make their way to America?"

Maeve grinned at Charlotte, who was sitting two desks away. Charlotte, who was new to Brookline and to Abigail Adams this year, had lived all over the world with her father, who was a travel writer. It was all so exotic. Last year they'd lived on a houseboat on the Seine in Paris. The year before that, it was Port Douglas, Australia—and before that, the Serengeti desert in Africa. But Maeve suddenly realized that she really didn't know much about Charlotte's mother and where she came from. Finally, an assignment that was actually going to be fun! Who knows? Maybe Charlotte's mother was a princess or something and maybe somebody, somebody like herself, had an actress somewhere deep in their background. That would be so outrageous!

Ms. O'Reilly's voice brought Maeve back to reality. "Each of you," she continued, "needs to find three objects that you can bring in to class to create your own display. Each object should reveal something important about your family. Something that represents what kind of history your family has lived through and what interesting things might have happened to them along the way. Ms. Rodriguez and I are teaming up, so she'll be working with you on this project in English class as well. You'll each write a brief report on what you've learned and give a presentation to the class in three weeks."

Betsy Fitzgerald cleared her throat, her hand up in the air—again. "What if you're not really from anywhere?" she asked plaintively. "What if your family has *always* lived in America?"

"Well," Ms. O'Reilly said with a smile, "we all come from somewhere, Betsy. I'll help you do some research and find out more about your family. But remember, history doesn't necessarily have to be about immigration. Some of you may have grandparents who served in a war. Or who started a company. Or who did something else that you're very proud of. Find out all you can about your family's history by talking to your relatives. Your first task is to think. What are you curious about? Which members of your family do you want to talk to? After you've learned more, choose three objects that represent that history to share with the rest of us." The bell rang, and Ms. O'Reilly gave them a parting wave as she gathered up her materials and left the room.

Anna snapped her notebook shut, rolled her eyes, and gave Joline "the look." Anna ALWAYS looked scornful. Maeve couldn't remember the last assignment Anna hadn't groaned about. And talk about acting as though she didn't have any history! Anna and Joline were way too cool to acknowledge anything that had happened more than five minutes ago. They acted like they'd *always* been in seventh grade. The mere mention of being younger seemed to humiliate them. Maeve had a sudden recollection of Anna years earlier, in first grade. She hadn't always been super-cool. As Maeve grinned at the memory of Anna, front teeth missing, lopsided grin, Anna looked at her as if to say, "What's so funny, not-cool person?" Maeve still had a snapshot of Anna from that grade, back when they used to trade class photos. She had one of Joline, too. She bet neither of them would be eager for anyone to see those photos now. Maybe she should bring the pictures to school, Maeve mused. But her better self won out. Even if it was Anna and Joline, it would be so mean to embarrass them that way.

"Don't worry, Anna," Dillon said with a grin. "Just bring in a few shopping bags from the mall. That ought to cover it. Anna and Joline's history—in the bag!" Maeve giggled. So funny. Dillon was definitely one cool guy.

Anna flipped her hair back with a scowl. "What a lame assignment," she retorted. "Who cares about the past? Hasn't Ms. O'Reilly ever heard the phrase 'that's history'? It means over. Done with. THROUGH."

"I think the assignment sounds awesome," Avery piped up. Avery, who'd been adopted from Korea when she was a baby, loved the idea of finding out more about her own history, and she wasn't going to keep quiet just because Anna and Joline were trying to act too cool for words. "Are you actually afraid you might learn something new, Anna?" she asked. One of the few people in their class who was not intimidated by the Queens of Mean, Avery just grinned broadly when Anna glared at her.

"I know what I'm bringing in," Pete Wexler announced. "A football, a baseball, and a hockey stick."

"I think this is actually supposed to be about your *family*, dude," Dillon said, grabbing his books. "And not just about YOU. Plus it's supposed to be about the past, not about the present."

"What about an OLD football?" Pete asked.

Everyone was talking about the assignment as they gathered up their things. "I don't even know where my dad's family comes from," Abby Ross was saying to Katani as the girls headed out the door.

"I think this assignment could be really interesting," Isabel said, her dark eyes shining. "I would really like to learn more about my grandparents' life in Mexico. I mean, I love to visit them and eat my abuelita's cooking, but I never really asked them a lot of questions about their past. My grandfather loves to tell stories, so I know he'll really like this assignment. I might even draw some cartoons or something," Isabel enthused.

Katani nodded. "I bet you could do a really great project, Isabel. You are such a good artist, your display will be fantastic. There's a lot of stuff I've wanted to know about my family background too, but you know how it is ... you just never get around to asking. I think I'll interview my grandmother."

Katani's grandmother, Mrs. Fields, was the principal of Abigail Adams Junior High. Everybody in Brookline thought she was the greatest. All the kids liked her because she was so calm, nice, and fair. There were so many things that weren't fair, Maeve mused, like having to go to school on sunny days, having to go to bed before nine thirty during the week even if there was a great movie on, and having to put up with an annoying little brother. It was very reassuring to know that the principal of your school was fair.

Katani said her grandmother had lived in Brookline all of her life. Katani knew a few things about her grandmother's life in the 1950s and 1960s, but she was eager to learn more. Mrs. Fields had lived through the civil rights movement and often talked about the time she saw Martin Luther King, Jr. come to preach at her family's church. She also thought that her grandmother had been part of some bus ride or protest march. Katani said she was going to interview her grandmother like they were on NBC News or something. Maeve could just see Katani preparing for the interview. "Katani, I bet you'll even dress up in a suit like a newscaster."

Katani gave Maeve a huge grin. "You know I will, girl. Looking professional goes hand in hand with being professional." Maeve, Avery, Charlotte, and Isabel all laughed in unison. Katani was so going to have her own business some day.

As Maeve slid her laptop into her book bag, she started thinking about her mom and dad and what different worlds they came from. Her father's family, like Ms. O'Reilly's, had come from Ireland. His parents had come to America after World War II when they were only sixteen years old. They met on the boat coming over. Nana Mary and Grandpa Tom still had their Irish accents. Maeve loved to listen to them talk.

Her mother's family had come from Eastern Europe—Maeve wasn't exactly sure which country. She knew her parents used to tease each other about how different their backgrounds were. It went along with the differences in their temperaments. Maeve's father was a cheerful, relaxed man who loved taking life easy. He always joked that he was well suited for running the Movie House, because he loved nothing better than enjoying himself and watching other people have a good time. He had a favorite motto: "Art is the key to understanding life." Maeve's mother was more the driven type. She'd gone to New York University and majored in English. She'd taught high school for a few years before she got married. Once she had kids, she stayed home and never had a job, outside of helping in the cinema. She was an organizer fiend. Maeve's mom could be really fun, but she was much stricter than her dad. Maybe some of this had to do with her background, Maeve thought. Well, she was going to have a lot of learning to do for this project.

"Hey! What if I discover a famous actress in my family's past?" she said, grabbing her things as she followed her friends to the cafeteria. "Wouldn't that be cool? Maybe I'm actually related to some awesome old celebrity. Like Audrey Hepburn or Greta Garbo!"

All the Beacon Street Girls laughed. It was clear that Maeve had Hollywood in her veins. She knew the words to every song in every movie ever made. And whenever they were in a jam, Maeve could recite the perfect movie line to fit the occasion. Her personal favorite was "Life is like a box of chocolates; you never know what you're gonna get," from *Forrest Gump*. When she wasn't watching movies, Maeve loved reading about them. Every time she passed a magazine stand she had to grab the latest celebrity magazine. This meant that she knew every bit of Hollywood gossip ... much to Avery's amazement and occasional disgust. "How can you read that stuff, Maeve? It's so ridiculous. I mean who cares about who's marrying who for twelve minutes?" ranted Avery.

Katani came to Maeve's defense. "It's research, Avery. Maeve has to learn about the field she wants to succeed in. I read fashion and business magazines. It would be kind of silly if Maeve read all about fruit flies and how they multiply." Katani was the only one who could get Avery to calm down sometimes.

If it were up to her, Maeve would gladly spend every afternoon taking voice lessons or working on dance moves. But her mom had different ideas. Her mom's plan for Maeve was Hebrew class two days a week and tutoring with Matt Kierney. And to Maeve's disappointment, hip-hop dance class had been dropped until she brought her grades back up. But Maeve was an optimist. She was sure she'd be back to dance in a matter of weeks.

"It's funny. Dad and I have traveled so much, but I don't think I know that much about where his family comes from," Charlotte wondered out loud. "I mean, I know they were from England a long time ago. But I don't even know exactly where."

"I hope it wasn't Oxford," Avery said with a grin. Everyone giggled. The memory of the girls' last adventure was still fresh in their minds. Charlotte's father had been offered a teaching position in Oxford, England, and it had taken all five of the Beacon Street Girls to convince him to stay put and to give Charlotte a chance at her dream—to spend her junior high and high school years in the U.S.

Charlotte was really looking forward to the Heritage Museum project. She loved research and writing, and she was curious about her family and its past. Her mother had died when she was young, leaving Charlotte with lots of unanswered questions about her background. Maybe, like Maeve, she would learn more about herself in the process. "Who knows?" she mused. "There might even have been an astronomer in our family." Charlotte loved science almost as much as writing. *Stars and books*, she liked to say ... those were her two best friends.

"I've got a triple-header research project," Avery added thoughtfully. "I've got my mom's history and my dad's. But I've also got my own." She grinned. "It's going to be cool, finding out more about where I really came from." Avery loved challenges, and with her usual blunt, go-for-it manner, she was looking forward to this one.

It was clear this assignment was going to give all of the Beacon Street Girls a lot to think about in the coming weeks. There was a great deal they were all going to learn about themselves and about each other.

CHAPTER

2

Up for Grabs

The menu for school lunch was posted on a small board at the beginning of the lunch line. Today's special was something called "mystery subs."

"Lunch," Avery announced, peering at the sandwiches wrapped in plastic on top of the cafeteria counter, "is NOT a place where anyone wants mystery." She took a sandwich, but she didn't look happy about it. "My mom usually makes me a super protein wrap, but she had a meeting this morning and left Scott and me to fend for ourselves. And you should have seen Scott. He was acting like he was the president, ordering me around. I bolted out of there fast." Avery and her brother Scott, who was sixteen, lived with their mom about a mile away from school. Her older brother Tim was off at college in Vermont. Avery's parents were divorced, and her dad lived in Colorado. Avery got to see a lot of her father over vacations, but during the school year they had to rely on e-mail and the telephone to keep in touch.

Charlotte grinned. Avery was definitely not the cooking maestro. "Fending for herself" clearly meant scooping some

✿ 17 ✿

money out of an emergency stash and standing in the cafeteria lunch line. Charlotte, on the other hand, had made lunch for herself today. She was just in line to keep her friends company and to buy a drink. "Avery, have you ever thought about actually making your own lunch?" she asked, helping herself to a bottle of juice. "Or thought about learning to *cook*? It's kind of fun!"

Avery shuddered. "No thank you. Lunch is something to pick up from the kitchen counter and put in my backpack," she said cheerfully. "My mom knows exactly what I like. A turkey wrap sandwich, popcorn, granola bars ... She's got it down to a science. Why mess with perfection?" She looked uneasily at the "mystery sub" on her tray. "I need power food at lunch, remember?"

Of the five Beacon Street Girls, Avery was by far the most athletic. There wasn't a ball Avery didn't like. And, although soccer was her current obsession, she was good in pretty much every sport she tried, even basketball. Though Avery was one of the shortest girls in the seventh grade, she was consistently the high scorer on the basketball team. It just proved that being tall wasn't the only advantage on the court—Avery was super-speedy and could dribble past anybody. Given all the energy she put into her games, Avery needed a lot of fuel. And, she loved eating—but cooking was another story. "Cook away, Charlotte," she said now, helping herself to a granola bar. "I'm always happy to sample whatever you make!"

Charlotte grinned. "I just signed up for some cooking classes with my dad," she told her friends. "The Community Center is running a six-week class on Saturday mornings, and it looks really fun. I want to expand my repertoire beyond Croque-Monsieurs, brownies, and eggs à la Charlotte."

"I don't know," Maeve said. "I'm kind of with you, Avery,

on this one. Doesn't cooking take tons of time?" Maeve's idea of the perfect snack was picking up a cupcake from Party Favors on her way home from school. Or a bagful of Swedish Fish from Irving's Toy and Card Shop. Of course, best of all was getting a frozen hot chocolate at Montoya's, the bakery on Harvard Street that was the seventh-grade hangout after school.

Charlotte shook her head. "The class looks great," she told them. "Guess what our first recipe is going to be?" When no one answered, she told them. *Chocolate fondue.* "It looks unbelievable," Charlotte said. "And it's totally delicious. You just chop up all your favorites—bananas, strawberries, marshmallows, pretzels—and dip them in hot fudge."

"Now *that* sounds like something worth learning," Avery admitted.

Everyone looked impressed, and Maeve had to concede that melting chocolate might be a worthy cooking exercise in its own right. By the time the girls had claimed their favorite table near the lunchroom window, the conversation had turned back to the social studies project.

"I bet someone in my past was an animal lover. Maybe they ran a zoo or something," Avery said, finishing off her granola bar. "If I find out that's true, can I bring Marty in for part of my Heritage Museum?"

The girls groaned. Avery was so crazy about animals. She was the one who had first discovered Marty, the adorable dog that the girls collectively adopted. Half-hidden in the bushes in the park across from Charlotte's house, Marty had managed to capture all the girls' hearts. And while Avery had begged and begged her mother to let her keep him, Avery's mom refused. Dogs made her eyes run and her skin break out in hives. So, Marty lived with Charlotte.

"Poor Avery," chimed in Katani. "Settling for reptiles as pets ... Have some of my animal crackers—they'll make you'll feel better."

Never one to turn down food, Avery snatched the animal crackers out of Katani's hand and popped them in her mouth. "Thanks, Katani. Someday I hope you will grow to love Walter and Frogster as much as I do. Think of it this way. Walter eats rodents and Frogster eats bugs, both of which you detest!"

"Avery," piped in Maeve. "I don't think Katani is ever going to change her mind about snakes and frogs. And I kind of agree with her. Furry pets are so much cuter and cuddlier."

Charlotte gave Maeve a look from across the table. Suddenly, Maeve realized what she had said. "Avery, I am *so* sorry. I know you want a furry pet really badly. I just forget sometimes and things pop out of my mouth."

"That's all right, Maeve. It's just so unfair," Avery complained. "You know, they've done RESEARCH on this kind of thing. Furry pets are really good for your blood pressure and stuff like that. Maybe if I told my mother I would be better adjusted if I had a REAL pet to take care of, that would change things ..."

DON'T FORGET THE DOG!

Suddenly, Charlotte clapped her hand to her forehead. "I almost forgot, you guys. My dad wants to take me to New York this weekend. He's got a writing conference to go to at NYU, and he said I can come with him. We might even get to see a play together."

"Broadway!" Maeve swooned. "Char, you are SO lucky." She started ticking off the plays she wanted to see—and it was a long list. "And you've GOT to go to the Radio and TV Museum. I love that place. Nana Mary and Grandpa Tom took Sam and me there once. It was awesome. You get to be on TV and everything."

"No—go to Wall Street! You can get a tour of the stock exchange, then hop over to Soho and check out all the street vendors. My cousin says you can find the best designer bags for really cheap!" Katani exclaimed. Fashion queen that she was, Katani had just become interested in the stock market. It had started as a game with her mother. The two of them had been scouring the stock pages for the past few months to see if they could find some winners.

"I've never been to New York," Isabel said wistfully. "I hear that the Metropolitan Museum of Art is to die for." Isabel, who loved everything having to do with art—from painting to collage to cartooning—had already fallen in love with the Boston Museum of Fine Arts. She had seen a Gauguin and Monet exhibit, and couldn't wait to see the new photography exhibit at the Institute of Contemporary Art. Her eyes lit up at the very thought of two days of museum hopping in New York. "I want to live in the city someday," she said. "Maybe I'll be a famous artist and you all can come to my opening at some amazing gallery."

"We'll be there," enthused Maeve. "And, we'll be your most loyal fans. Right, girls?" Katani, Charlotte, and Avery nodded vigorously in agreement.

"Just stay away from Yankee Stadium," Avery advised, referring to her beloved Red Sox's archrivals.

Charlotte laughed. It was so funny to hear her friends' reactions—clearly each having very different ideas about how she should spend her weekend! "There's only one problem," she told them. "What am I going to do with Marty while we're away? It's only for two days and one night, but he can't possibly stay by himself."

There was silence as everyone thought about this. Marty was adored by all the girls, even Katani, who was an admitted "kitty-kat girl."

"I guess he can't really go with you," Katani said.

"The hotel doesn't take dogs," Charlotte told her. "Besides, how am I supposed to go to all the places you're recommending with Marty in tow?"

"Marty, the traveling dog," Isabel giggled. "Just picture him hopping up the steps of the Met."

"Marty does Wall Street," Katani added with a grin. "He'd need a tie, of course. And a briefcase."

"No, better yet," Avery blurted. "Keep him in a doggie sport tote, with his head popping out every once in a while!"

"Very Elle Woods," mused Maeve.

"Why can't Miss Pierce take care of him?" Avery asked. The Ramseys lived in a big yellow house on Summit Avenue—a two-family Victorian that they shared with Sapphire Pierce, their landlady. She was retired from her lifelong career as an astronomer. She and Charlotte loved having tea together sometimes in the afternoons. Charlotte was fascinated by her work on the Hubble telescope, and Miss Pierce liked hearing about the same junior high school where she'd been a student years ago. Miss Pierce was fond of Marty, and it seemed like a good suggestion.

But Charlotte was shaking her head. "She can't take care of Marty this weekend. We already checked with her," she said. "She's got something going on and she said she was going to be too busy to look after him."

The five girls looked at each other, concerned. Katani frowned. "What's she doing? She is always ready to take care of Marty. Is she sick?"

"No, I don't think so," answered Charlotte. "She just

couldn't do it. I have to admit I was a little curious myself. I thought maybe she was going on a trip or something, but she's so shy and hasn't been anywhere for so long. The whole thing is a little strange."

"I'd love to take Marty," Isabel piped in. "But Aunt Lourdes is NOT a pet person. I think it's hard enough for her, sharing her apartment with Mom and Elena Maria and me." Isabel's young aunt, a nurse, was helping to take care of Isabel and her ninth-grade sister, and guiding Isabel's mother through treatment for her multiple sclerosis. "You know how strict Aunt Lourdes is, and what a neat freak too," Isabel added. "Besides, we barely have enough room for the four of us. Marty would have to stay in the closet." All of them howled at the vision of Marty in a closet. There would be nothing left standing after Marty had his way. Plus, Marty would be too lonely. He loved to be held and cuddled, and he was used to sleeping with Charlotte—sometimes sneaking under the covers on a cold night. Poor Marty!

"Count me out, too," Katani said with a sigh. "My mom wants us all to head up to visit Candice at college this weekend." She shook her head. "You know my sister. She's already been voted MVP of her field hockey team and she's barely been there one season. Mom wants to take Patrice, Kelley, and me up there to watch her game."

The Summers were a very tight family, and they often did things together on the weekends.

Everyone turned to Maeve. "I can't," Maeve said. "My mom says she has an interview, I'm not sure what for, but she asked me to look after Sam in the afternoon." Spending time with Sam, her pesky little brother, was not exactly her favorite thing to do. She made a face. "Besides, dogs freak Sam out. Go figure—he'll watch the goriest war movie ever made, but when he SEES a dog, he acts like a basket case."

Charlotte was looking worried. "Okay," she said finally. "Maybe Miss Pierce will have an idea of someone who can dog-sit. Or my dad can ask around in his department at B.U. There must be someone who can watch him."

Avery couldn't stand the thought of this a minute longer. "We can't let a perfect stranger watch Marty. You know how sensitive he is ... *I'll* take care of him!"

"Avery," Katani said warningly. "Your mom's allergic."

"And," Charlotte pointed out, "didn't she say *no* when you asked if you could have Marty at your house before?"

"What if I put him in the carriage house? She never goes in there," Avery said.

The girls exchanged glances.

"I don't know, Avery. We don't want you to get in trouble with your mom. Right?" asked Charlotte, looking toward Katani.

"I'll keep him hidden. We don't really use our carriage house, so I can make a bed for him in there," Avery insisted. When everyone looked questioningly at her, she added, "I promise. He won't be in anyone's way. Anyway, my mom isn't even going to be around much this weekend! She's got lots of meetings. She's planning some kind of big fund-raising event for that boarding school she went to when she was in high school." Avery's voice sounded teary. "Come on, guys. Just this once—let me take him!"

The girls looked uncertainly at each other. Avery was so head over heels in love with Marty that she couldn't always be rational when it came to making plans about him. But they could see that Avery was near tears and that was so unlike her. Avery was tough; she never cried about anything. But Marty was special. After all, she was the one who insisted that all the girls adopt him.

"Avery," Charlotte said slowly. "What if your mother finds out and gets really mad at you, or at all of us?"

"First of all, she won't find out. Second of all, even if she does, she can't get mad because I won't keep him in the house, where his hair would bother her. Please, guys. Give me a chance. I'll keep him safe and out of the way in the carriage house. I'll walk him every day and snuggle with him and play Frisbee. It will be so great and Marty will be with someone who loves him."

Charlotte didn't know what to say. Nobody did. They had never seen Avery so ... so desperate for something. "Well, if you really think it'll be okay," she said at last.

None of the girls could think of a better plan. Someone needed to take care of Marty for the weekend. Maybe Avery was right. Marty hated going to the vet's and really—how much could possibly go wrong between Friday and Sunday evening?

Just then Nick Montoya walked by the girls' table. "Hey Charlotte, do you want to go over that Properties of Water experiment that's due tomorrow before science next period?" he asked casually.

Charlotte could feel her cheeks burn as Nick waited expectantly for an answer. "Sure. I'll meet you in the lab in a few minutes."

Charlotte and the other Beacon Street Girls watched him walk off. "Oh, this is so embarrassing," moaned Charlotte as she placed her hands on her pink cheeks. "I just can't stop blushing when I see him. It's a total curse!"

"Somebody needs to invent an anti-blush cream," stated Katani.

"You could call it Blush Free Forever or BFF for short," quipped Isabel.

Suddenly, Dillon and Pete Wexler rushed by the table. "Science lab now! Anna and Joline are chasing Henry Yurt around the lab. He dumped water on Anna's head, and she's melting!" he cackled in his best imitation of the Wicked Witch of the West.

Marty was completely forgotten for the moment as the girls and everybody around them ran to catch the drama in the lab. No one wanted to miss it. Luckily the girls were right by the door of the cafeteria because the Yurt versus Anna and Joline story was spreading like wildfire through the cafeteria. The halls were filled with kids running and laughing at the idea of the nerdiest kid in seventh grade being chased around science lab by the school's "coolest" girls.

Avery was the first of the Beacon Street Girls to reach the door. Nick Montoya was already leaning at the doorway—a big grin plastered on his face. Anna and Joline were standing to one side of the lab bench. Black streaks of mascara dripped down Anna's face, wet stringy hair ruining her perfect look. Both Anna and Joline were looking like they could take Henry Yurt and bury him alive. Mr. Richardson was glaring at Henry, who was standing on the other side of the lab bench.

Nick gestured to everyone in the hall to be quiet.

"Henry," Mr. Richardson said. "I think you need to apologize to Anna."

"I don't want an apology. I want to sue him. He's such an idiot. Everyone knows you were supposed to make sure the water was level!" yelled Anna.

"No name calling, Anna. Henry made a mistake. He needs to be more careful about his lab procedures. But first, he needs to apologize and then clean up this mess. Go ahead, Henry. Apologize to Anna."

Henry mumbled, "Sorry." He didn't sound like he meant it.

"That's not an apology," scowled Anna. "He's faking it."

"I agree, Anna."

There was a collective gasp in the room. Mrs. Fields had suddenly appeared and was sending all the kids who were peering into the room away.

The Beacon Street Girls were already in the room so they had to wait to file out. That meant they got to see and hear everything.

"Henry," continued Mrs. Fields. "I want to hear a real Abigail Adams apology."

Henry looked up. Nobody messed with a Mrs. Fields order. It just wasn't done. Resigned, Henry managed to squeak out, "Sorry, Anna, for spilling water on your head and making weird black streaks run down your face."

Both Mr. Richardson and Mrs. Fields looked like they swallowed something sour.

"Now Anna, you need to apologize to Henry for the name calling."

Anna put her hand on her hips and looked at Mrs. Fields with disbelief. She looked like she was about to say "No way." But Mrs. Fields's raised eyebrow seemed to make her change her mind.

In a sickeningly sweet voice she said, "I am sorry, Henry, for calling you an idiot. It's not your fault that you can't follow directions and get your act together."

Mr. Richardson sent Henry on his way, and Mrs. Fields took Anna to her office for cleanup. As Henry walked down the hall, everyone chanted in low tones, "Yurt, Yurt, Yurt." Henry Yurt would now and forever remain a legend at Abigail Adams Junior High.

CHAPTER

3

Nominated

A.M. WEIRDNESS

Maeve's mom was acting strange on Friday morning.
Usually, she was the only one in the Kaplan-Taylor
household who had much energy before eight o'clock. But
this morning, she was just sitting with the newspaper spread
out in front of her at the kitchen table, looking blankly at the
headlines without really reading them. Sam and Maeve were
running around trying to get ready, but she wasn't jumping
up to help them the way she always did. Not even when Sam
freaked out about where he'd left his homework.

"Where's Daddy?" Maeve asked, pouring herself some
cereal.

"Still asleep," her mother said absently. "He had a film
festival that ran late last night."

Maeve glanced at her mother. Her voice sounded
weird—kind of muffled and distant, like she was thinking
about something else. Not her mother's style at all.

"Maeve? Sam?" her mother said, as Maeve and her little
brother were trying to cram everything they could remember

that they needed for school into their book bags. "Your dad and I want to take some time this weekend to have a family talk. Can you be sure to be around on Saturday, around dinnertime?"

Maeve stared at her mom. Since when did they make family plans on a Saturday evening? Wasn't that prime time for hanging out with friends?

"Uh ... I don't know, Mom," she began. But she stopped when she saw the look on her mother's face. Clearly this was something serious.

"Nobody's sick, are they, Mom?" asked Maeve nervously.

"No, honey. No one is sick. But we all need to talk."

"Okay," Maeve said. Whatever this was, it sounded non-negotiable.

But what could be going on? What kind of talk did they all need to have?

"How serious?" she asked, suddenly curious.

Her mom wasn't going to talk about it now, though. That much was clear. "Maeve, it's time for school. You'll be late! We'll talk this weekend," she said.

Not really reassuring, Maeve thought. She could've just said *No, nothing serious*, and Maeve would've been relieved, and that would be that.

Now she had to go off to school wondering what on earth was the matter. Parents could be so frustrating sometimes.

Daydreams and Prizes

Isabel, Maeve, Katani, Charlotte, and Avery met at their lockers before homeroom to discuss plans for the big "Marty-Drop." The girls were going to bring Marty to Avery's house on Friday evening. "We'll meet you at your back door and help you get him set up in the carriage house," Katani said.

"I've got all his stuff to bring, too. His water bowl, his leash ..." Charlotte began.

"But we'll have to hide him in something in case anyone's around," Maeve pointed out.

"Put him in my soccer bag," Avery instructed.

"Won't he suffocate in that thing?" Isabel demanded.

"I didn't mean to zip it up," Avery retorted, laughing.

Finally, they had a plan: that evening the four girls would bring Marty and his things over. Marty, the little stowaway, would be hidden in Avery's soccer bag—unzipped. Meanwhile Avery would set up a warm spot for him in the carriage house, and with any luck, Avery's mother would be none the wiser—no sneezing or hives, no trace of dog.

The homeroom bell rang, and everyone made their way into Ms. Rodriguez's classroom, still talking about Marty and how to keep a hyper dog out of sight for a whole weekend. Avery was so excited she could hardly contain herself for the rest of the day. Maeve slid into her desk, taking out her laptop. She was having a hard time concentrating. She was getting more and more preoccupied by what her mom had said. The big family discussion planned for Saturday seemed to be weighing on her mom's mind. And suddenly it was weighing on Maeve's, too.

What could be going on?

Maeve fiddled with her pen. It was her favorite—bright pink, with a long feathery plume. Maybe she was the problem. Maeve and her mother hadn't been getting along so well lately. Maeve's grades had suffered this year. Seventh grade was so much harder than sixth! It seemed that one week she would do really well in history and then the next week she would forget an assignment. And lately, there'd been friction at home over her grades. Her mom wanted her to be more organized. Her dad, on the other hand, thought Maeve's mom was too hard on her. He thought—

"Maeve," Ms. Rodriguez said, with the gentle firmness that suggested it wasn't the first time she'd said her name. "Are you with us?"

Maeve sat bolt upright, knocking her pen off her desk and onto the floor. A few people laughed, including Anna and Joline. Maeve could feel her cheeks redden. "Uh, sure. I'm—I was just ..." Maeve sat up straighter. "Could you repeat the question?" she asked, trying to ignore the superior glance that Betsy was giving her. Betsy Fitzgerald, of course, would never daydream in class. Maeve snatched her pen by its feathery plume, ignoring Betsy's frown.

"I was just saying," Ms. Rodriguez continued with a smile, "there is a community service award being given in Brookline. They're looking for nominations for students who have made special contributions to their communities. And I wanted to let you and the whole class know, Maeve, that you've been nominated. Project Thread has made a real difference for the children at Jeri's Place, and the seventh-grade teachers at Abigail Adams have selected you and your project to represent our school."

Maeve couldn't believe her ears. For a minute, she thought she was still daydreaming. But as she looked around at her friends' smiling faces, she realized that this was actually happening. Inside she was really proud of the way her blanket project had turned out. But she'd never expected to be nominated for an award because of it.

"Whoa, way to go, Maeve!" Avery called out, unable to contain her enthusiasm. On the other side of the room, Katani and Charlotte burst into applause. And behind

Charlotte, Isabel gave Maeve an enthusiastic thumbs-up.

"Speech! Speech!" yelled Dillon.

Maeve's blush deepened. She wasn't used to being singled out like this. The blanket project was something that she'd dreamed up one night, wondering what it would be like to be alone and cold, without best friends for consolation. When she grew up, Maeve was determined that she would *always* do something for homeless people. The thought of anyone, especially children, being homeless really bothered her.

Whoever would have believed this? Maeve thought now, looking across the homeroom at Katani and Isabel. Talk about proving that teamwork can get the job done! Once Katani stopped worrying about Isabel being a fifth wheel, she threw in her incredible organizational talent, and the blanket project really got off the ground.

"Ms. Rodriguez," Maeve said slowly, "I—thanks so much, that's so great, but I wanted to say that I don't think it should just be ME getting nominated. It took a whole group of us to get this to happen." She glanced appreciatively around the room at her friends.

Ms. Rodriguez nodded. "We talked about that, Maeve. The seventh-grade teachers really do want to acknowledge the whole group of you who gave your study hall second period to get this wonderful project off the ground. But Maeve, you're the one who came up with the idea. You spearheaded the project, and your vision carried it through. You should be very proud," she added, her dark eyes sparkling. "There'll be a ceremony at the Community Center next Friday evening at seven o'clock. The winners will be announced then. So everyone, I hope you'll all come out to support Maeve and our school. Good luck, Maeve!"

Everyone clapped, and Maeve could feel her heart pounding.

The bell rang, signaling that homeroom was over. Maeve's fingers were trembling as she tried to get her laptop into her book bag. She couldn't believe it. In all her years of school, Maeve had never been nominated for anything. She could sing and dance, but she'd never been honored for a school project before. Usually when her name got called, it meant that she'd probably forgotten her homework. This was GOOD news. Wait until her mom and dad heard about this—they'd be so proud of her. Maybe it would even pick her mother's spirits up!

"Way to go, Kaplan-Taylor! You blanket-making goddess," Avery cried, thumping Maeve on her back as the girls congregated outside of homeroom.

Maeve giggled as Avery's friendly thwack almost knocked her into Katani. Avery wasn't exactly a delicate flower, despite her diminutive stature.

"This calls for a celebration. Montoya's, after school!" Katani said, putting her arm around Maeve and giving her a squeeze.

Maeve had the vague feeling that she was supposed to be somewhere after school. "Just a sec," she said, rummaging around in her book bag for her day planner. Darn—she'd left it at home, on her dresser. She couldn't remember what, if anything, she had planned. Didn't she have an appointment or lesson after school today?

She couldn't remember. If she had somewhere else to be, she'd figure it out later.

"Okay," she said happily, linking arms with Katani and Isabel. "Montoya's it is!"

Katani was right. This was something to celebrate.

"Okay, guys. Grab a table and let's splurge," Isabel cried, pushing through the door to Montoya's that afternoon. "The sky's the limit!" She opened up her wallet and a shadow crossed her face. "Katani," she whispered, grabbing her arm. "Can we split this? I thought I had more money, but I've only got three dollars!"

"No problem. I've got my baby-sitting money," Katani whispered back.

It was Friday afternoon, and the popular bakery was crowded with junior high students. Most of the tables were taken, but the Beacon Street Girls found one in the corner. They waved at people they knew and maneuvered their way up to the counter to order drinks. Nick Montoya and his sister Fabiana were helping out in the café after school, and Nick took everyone's orders. He gave Charlotte a special smile when she ordered her drink. Katani gave her a nudge. Lately, Nick had been paying a lot of attention to Charlotte, and she knew her friends were starting to notice. Charlotte wasn't sure about Nick as a boyfriend yet. But he was nice ... *really* nice. He'd make a good friend.

A few minutes later, they were all sitting down, sipping iced hot chocolate and munching on pastries.

"Here's to Maeve," Charlotte said, lifting her glass.

"No one I know has ever won an award before," Isabel said admiringly, taking a bite of a buñuelo, one of the café's specialties.

"I haven't won yet," Maeve pointed out, taking a delicate bite of her cookie. She pushed her red curls back, frowning thoughtfully. "I wonder how they're going to do this. Do you suppose they'll hand out awards? And what should I wear? D'you think it'll be super-dressy?"

Katani grinned. "Kind of like the Oscars?"

Maeve grinned. "Okay, okay. I guess this is a little different," she admitted. But she was SO excited. "Should I write a speech—just in case?" she asked.

"I could help you," Charlotte offered.

"And I could help with figuring out what to wear," Katani added.

Just then, the door to Montoya's swung open and Anna and Joline came sauntering in. Anna had one arm flung casually around Joline's shoulder, in that "we are SO cool and such totally best friends" way that she had. It was amazing. Even the now-famous lab incident didn't affect their coolness. Anna and Joline almost always dressed alike. If it weren't for the fact that Anna was taller and blonde, you'd almost think they were clones. They managed to wear everything with an attitude that suggested that if it wasn't a trend yet, it would be by the end of the day. Today, they weren't dressed identically, but the effect was pretty much the same. Tight, low-rider jeans. Form-fitting T-shirts, and scrunchy terry-cloth sweatshirts, halfway unzipped. They walked up to the counter together to place their orders—water.

Katani looked incredulous. "WATER at Montoya's! What a waste," she muttered.

"Sshhhh," Maeve said. Anna and Joline were walking back from the counter, right toward their table.

"Hey, Maeve," Anna said lazily, raising one eyebrow and looking intently at Maeve, totally ignoring Charlotte, Isabel, Katani, and Avery. She was making it very clear that she was interested in talking ONLY to Maeve. "Pretty cool about that award thingy you're getting."

"Yeah," Joline echoed, flicking her long brown hair back with one finger. "Nice going, Maeve."

Maeve swallowed. She wasn't used to having the Queens of Mean bother to talk to her—let alone go out of their way to come over and say hi. "I haven't actually won yet—" she began. But Anna and Joline didn't seem to notice.

"It's cool," Anna continued. "Who knows? Maybe you'll be famous."

Okay ... when was the backhanded compliment coming? Maeve wondered.

"We're sitting over there," Joline said, gesturing over to a table filled with eighth graders. "If you want, you can come sit with us." She made it sound like she'd just offered Maeve a chance to visit Mount Olympus and become immortal.

Maeve glanced around the table. Nobody said anything. Her friends' expressions were impossible to read. Maeve was surprised by the attention, and she couldn't help feeling a tiny bit flattered. She couldn't remember the last time Anna or Joline had asked her anything.

Maybe she'd misjudged them. Maybe they really weren't that horrible after all.

On the other hand, Anna and Joline hadn't exactly included the rest of her friends in the invitation. They'd clearly been talking just to her. That made Maeve feel a little uncomfortable—her personal mantra was always "the more the merrier." She didn't accept invitations if they didn't include all her friends, too.

"Maybe later," she said noncommittally. She glanced up at Anna. "Or you guys could come sit with US," she suggested. That seemed like the perfect solution! All-inclusive, just the way Maeve liked.

Avery nudged her under the table. Clearly she wasn't exactly excited by the idea of having Anna and Joline join them.

Anna looked at Joline. "Uh ... thanks, but we already put our stuff over there," she said. Translation: We are WAY TOO COOL to sit with you guys.

"Okay," Maeve said with one of her "fine with me" shrugs.

Anna and Joline exchanged glances. Clearly they weren't used to inviting someone to join them and being told "maybe." But Maeve was having a good time right where she was, and she didn't feel like moving ... especially since Dillon had just come through the door. And if Maeve moved to join ANYONE, it sure wasn't going to be Anna and Joline!

Peacocks are SO attitudinal!

Isabel M.

CHAPTER

4

Double Trouble

SOMETHING'S UP ... BUT WHAT?

"Hey! Anyone home?" Maeve called out, stuffing her keys back into her backpack as she let herself into the narrow front hallway. The Kaplan-Taylors' duplex apartment above the Brookline Movie House was really cool. The apartment had high ceilings and lots of charm, but not as much space as Maeve would have liked. The hallway was especially cramped. She practically tripped over Sam's backpack, which he'd left right in the middle of the floor. Three biographies of General Patton and a shoebox full of toy soldiers spilled over onto the floor.

Sam had absolutely no respect for Maeve's privacy—he even read her I.M. messages when she wasn't looking. Not to mention, he also had a pretty suspect sense of personal hygiene. Ugh—those grubby fingernails! Maeve shuddered. On top of that, his obsession with everything military, especially if it involved some obscure historical war that nobody else had heard of, was seriously annoying. Like who knew all the battles of the Peloponnesian Wars? Sam, that's who. He had a huge laminated map covering one entire wall of his bedroom. He loved sticking little pins in it and pretending that he was a military tactician, mapping out a new battle scheme.

Maeve had never even heard of some of the countries Sam kept pretending to invade. And she couldn't see why on earth he'd want to read about WAR all the time. Well, sometimes he liked to read about viruses and other creepy stuff, too. *Boys*, she thought with exasperation. How could they start out like this and end up so totally cute? Dillon—had he ever been a grubby eight-year-old? Ms. O'Reilly was right, this history business was more complicated than it seemed.

Of course, Sam's teachers loved him. He got every answer right on every test without cracking a book, and he seemed like he'd learned how to read in his sleep. Most annoying of all, he was an ace speller. He could spell ANYTHING, even the names of those creepy generals he was obsessed with. Sometimes it was hard to believe that the two of them were even related. He owned exactly two sweat-shirts, two pairs of pants—both hideous brown—and exactly one pair of shoes—and those were light-up sneakers. How uncool. He was positively fashion-impaired. As Maeve clambered up the steep staircase that led from the hallway up into their apartment, she scooped up some of her brother's stuff as she went. *There*. Another good deed for the day, she congratulated herself. Maybe Sam couldn't help being a whiz kid and a slob. She vowed to be nicer to him tonight. Maybe she'd even let him read her one of his World War II comic strips. She had to admit some of them were pretty interesting. Except the ones on Hitler. That crazy guy was just too scary for words.

Maeve heard voices as she approached the landing. Her

parents—that was strange, Maeve thought, checking her watch. Why wasn't her father still downstairs at the cinema? She opened the door into the kitchen, and sure enough, both her mom and dad were there. From the look on their faces she could tell that something was definitely wrong. Her mom was standing over near the fridge, her arms crossed and a frown on her face. Her dad was sitting at the kitchen table, fiddling with a paper clip. Both looked up at Maeve, but then her father looked away. He was obviously uncomfortable.

"Maeve," her mother said, with a funny sound in her voice that Maeve had never really heard before. She didn't sound disappointed or annoyed. Something else was going on. She actually sounded almost—sad. "Where were you this afternoon?"

"I was—" Maeve stopped short, setting her stuff down. "I went to Montoya's with my friends. We were talking about our new social studies project," she added quickly, trying to make it sound more like a study break than just hanging out.

"You were supposed to go over to work on your math homework with Matt, remember?" her mother asked. "He called here about half an hour ago, wondering where you were."

Maeve winced. Oh no! So that was the appointment she'd half-remembered. Matt Kierney had only been her tutor for a few weeks. He went to Boston College and Maeve thought he was great—smart, serious, but really nice.

"Shoot—I totally forgot!" she cried, smacking her forehead. "I left my planner upstairs. I KNEW there was something on for this afternoon, but I couldn't remember what it was."

Maeve waited for her mom to reprimand her. Usually, her mother got upset about this kind of thing.

But surprisingly, her mother didn't seem angry. Instead, she just looked a little worn out. Like her mind was on something else.

"I'll call Matt and reschedule," Maeve volunteered.

Her mom nodded. The word "reschedule" didn't even seem to get her attention—and that was definitely not like her. Say the *schedule* word, and she'd have her gigantic wall calendar out, marking out the days in different colored pens. But not this afternoon. She seemed too preoccupied.

Maeve decided her parents needed cheering up. Why not lift their spirits by sharing her good news with them?

"Mom, Dad, you're not going to believe this," Maeve said, "but I got nominated today for a community service award for my blanket project!"

"Maeve—that's wonderful!" her mother exclaimed, her face brightening.

Her father jumped up to give her a bear hug—just at the moment that her mother leaned in to embrace her. Both of them pulled back, and her mother's face turned red.

Weird, Maeve thought. Definitely weird.

She dismissed it, though—who knew why parents did what they did?—and proceeded to fill them both in on all the details about the award. They were really eager to hear about it. In fact, Maeve thought they seemed almost TOO eager. They kept asking more and more questions. Who would be at the ceremony? How many kids had been nominated? Finally, Maeve ran out of answers. She hadn't won yet! Why was everyone jumping to conclusions?

She tried three separate times to escape to her room— she was dying to check I.M. and see who might be online. But they didn't seem to want her to leave the kitchen.

Maeve decided that they were overreacting to her news

because this wasn't exactly an everyday event. Probably, she guessed, her life was a lot more exciting than theirs. *Parents*, she thought fondly. They really didn't have much perspective, did they? But she finally had to tear herself away and leave them to their own devices. They were going to have to wait to hear more details about the nomination later—she had to feed her guinea pigs, and she had to be over at Charlotte's house to help pack Marty up in less than an hour.

Maeve's guinea pigs were both female, but Maeve liked giving them romantic names from movies and TV shows, which she changed every time she felt like it. This week they were "Romeo" and "Juliet." Maeve scooped them up to give them each a kiss. "Hi guinea babies," she said sweetly, tickling Juliet's tummy and letting both of them run around her room. They needed some exercise after a whole day trapped in their cage!

Home sweet home, Maeve thought, looking fondly around her. Maeve's room was what Katani had labeled a "pink-fest." Posters covered one half of the wall near her bed, including her latest "shrine to hotness," with the cutest guys in Hollywood cut out of magazines and taped to the wall. Maeve was a collector, and her shelves were crowded with memorabilia—trophies and ribbons from dance classes all the way back to kindergarten, pictures of her friends, worn and fuzzy stuffed animals, glass figurines ... "girly-girl" stuff, as Avery called it. Maeve loved every single bit of her room, even the ruffly pink canopy on her bed.

Ooops. There was her offending day planner, lying on her dresser where she'd left it. Maeve vowed to keep all her things in one place so she wouldn't forget an appointment again.

She flung herself across her bed with her laptop.

♥ ∙∙

```
Notes to Self:
1. BE MORE ORGANIZED, keep day planner
   with book bag!
2. More guinea pig food—we're almost out.
   New names for Romeo and Juliet??
3. Dress for Friday night. Blue for a
   change? Or stick with pink, like in my
   daydream?
4. New screenname? Luv2shop05? Thinkpink05?
5. Acceptance speech??? Or am I jinxing
   myself if I write one ahead of time?
```

The house was quiet when Maeve let herself out an hour later, ready for the Marty transport. Strangely quiet. Her mom and dad were still sitting together at the kitchen table, but neither of them seemed to be saying much to the other.

They looked glad to see her when Maeve crashed through the kitchen, grabbing a snack from the fridge on the way out.

Her mom wanted to know when she'd be back and if she had her cell phone. The usual.

Her father wanted to remind her that she was supposed to help him with the film festival tomorrow. AND help watch Sam.

"Yes, yes, yes," Maeve said.

"Oh, and Maeve. Don't forget about tomorrow evening," her mother said.

"I won't forget," Maeve assured her. She really didn't like this. What could possibly need this much buildup?

"Oh, and you guys, I need to talk to YOU, too," she added, as she backed out of the kitchen door into the hallway. "I need to find out about your histories—both of you. So start thinking about some good stories about how you grew up and where you both come from, okay? Ms. O'Reilly wants them to be REAL. We're doing this awesome Heritage Museum, and I need to find stuff that shows who we are as a family. So maybe you could think about how you each grew up and how different it was. Then I can interview you."

Her parents exchanged glances, but neither of them spoke. Fine, Maeve thought, as she bounded out the door. Don't all jump at once to help me with my project!

Something was definitely up, but they didn't seem to be mad at HER.

Maybe we're MOVING, Maeve thought excitedly. Her parents might have found a wonderful house right near where they were living now. One with huge closets and tons of space and a nice gigantic new bedroom for Maeve. *Now we are talking*, thought Maeve.

But no matter what was brewing, Maeve hoped for the best. She was the kind of girl who, given the chance, always believed that the glass was half full, and not half empty. Lemonade out of lemons—that was her motto.

Marty Incognito

"He keeps WRIGGLING," Katani complained. "You guys, you have to be organized about this stuff!" She was trying valiantly to fit Marty's leash and toys in a neat coil inside his water bowl, and Isabel started to giggle.

"You really are a neat freak," Isabel said with amusement.

"I can't help it," Katani retorted. "I just like keeping things together. If you shared a bedroom as small as mine, you'd be super-organized, too."

"I DO share a small bedroom, remember? Only mine's a

mess. My sister's half probably looks like yours—neat as a pin." Isabel smiled. "My side looks like a tornado hit it."

The four girls were over at Charlotte's, up in the Tower, trying to pack Marty up for his secret weekend in Avery's carriage house.

"Okay, I think that's everything," Charlotte said at last. "He's got dog food, treats, toys, his bowls ... everything I can think of. Oops! Can't forget Happy Lucky Thingy—Marty can't be without his favorite chew toy." She bent down and picked up the pink chewy and stuffed it in the bag.

"You think he'll be okay in the carriage house all weekend?" Katani asked, worried. "What if it gets cold?"

It was autumn, and recently the temperature had dipped into the forties at night.

"Avery says the carriage house is pretty warm," Isabel pointed out. "Come on, guys. Let's walk Marty over on his leash, and when we get to the Maddens' we can squish him into the soccer bag. We don't want to get Avery's mom upset."

The girls followed Marty over to Avery's, which—as Charlotte pointed out—meant stopping at just about every bush and fire hydrant for a long sniff. As they got closer to Avery's, the houses got bigger and bigger, and the fences around them taller and taller. Avery lived in one of the most exclusive neighborhoods in town, and her house—a tall, stately colonial with pale gray shutters—looked even more imposing than usual as the girls walked up to the gate.

"Wow," exclaimed Isabel as she pointed to a maple tree. "Those leaves look like they are on fire." That was Isabel—always noting the color of things.

"Okay, little guy. In you go," Katani said cheerfully, stooping down and opening up Avery's soccer bag.

Marty sniffed it suspiciously and backed off, whimpering. He didn't look excited to jump inside.

"Put a treat inside the bag," Charlotte recommended.

In the end, that was the only way to coax Marty in. Once inside the bag, he started thrashing around wildly and barking. The girls looked at each other. They began laughing nervously.

"We kind of forgot about his sound effects," Maeve said.

"Why don't you ring the doorbell, Maeve? Ask Avery to come out here. We can't chance it, with him barking," Katani said.

Maeve looked at her. "What am I supposed to say? Why are we all showing up at Avery's on a Friday evening?"

"Improvise. You're good at that," Katani told her.

Maeve rang the doorbell, trying to think up a good story for Avery's mother. To her surprise, a guy answered the door—a CUTE guy, in fact. He looked like he was about sixteen or seventeen, with sandy-brown hair and freckles.

"Hey," Maeve said, staring. "Uh—is Avery here?"

He nodded. "AVERY," he yelled into the empty space of the room behind him.

Avery came thudding down the stairs, two at a time. "Hey," she said to Maeve, pushing her way past the cute guy. She looked closely at Maeve. "Why do you look like that? What are you staring at?"

"Who's he?" Maeve whispered.

"Scott, my *brother*," Avery said, disgusted. She paused, shaking her head at Maeve. "Don't even START, Maeve. He's OLD, for one thing. *And* he's got a girlfriend. *And* he's totally off-limits."

"I know. He's way too old for me," Maeve muttered. "I just didn't realize that was Scott, okay? He's a million times cuter than I remembered."

"Yeah, he got his braces off," Avery said with a shrug. "Come on, let's go get Marty settled before my mom comes back."

Avery—Maeve thought with a sigh—wouldn't know a cute guy if she tripped over one. Not even if she had one living under the same roof.

Well, Maeve might just have to make up a few excuses to come over and help look in on Marty. After all, a weekend was an awfully long time to leave a poor helpless little dog like Marty out there in the Maddens' carriage house!

It took almost half an hour to get Marty's bed set up in the corner. All the girls thought Avery had done an amazing job of getting the place ready for Marty. The place looked like a cool doggie apartment. She had piled up a ton of old blankets and had made a giant nest for him. She'd even laid out a row of new toys for him that she had bought with her allowance. The girls put his water bowl nearby, and his food dish, and hung his leash up on a hook.

"This looks great, Avery, but don't you think it's a little cold in here? Do you guys have a space heater?" Maeve asked. "I could go get it," she volunteered, picturing Scott helping her trek through the big house to find it.

"It's not safe to use a space heater. Those things cause fires. Besides, he's a dog. He'll be okay," Katani said. "We'll just tuck some extra blankets around him."

"Uh-oh! My mom's pulling into the driveway," Avery said quickly. "We better get going before she finds us."

"And you're *sure* she never uses the carriage house?" Katani asked for the dozenth time.

"I'm positive! Look at the place. It's just a giant-sized storage bin," Avery exclaimed. "Marty is going to be FINE. I promise. I love him. I will take the absolute best care of him.

I even bought a dog book. Look!" She held up a new paperback on the care and feeding of small dogs. "Now, go have a great time in New York, Charlotte. And the rest of you: DON'T WORRY." She dropped down to give Marty one more hug. "I promise to shower him with so much attention that he'll be spoiled rotten by the time Charlotte comes back for him on Sunday night!"

Reluctantly, the girls gave Marty a last hug good-night. Maeve thought he looked awfully tiny sitting all alone in that big old carriage house.

But Avery was firm. It was time for everyone to clear out. And time for Avery to indulge in her biggest dream—a weekend alone with her beloved borrowed, furry friend.

CHAPTER 5

The Perfect Family

"O K, kids. We need to talk," Maeve's mom said, taking a deep breath.

Here it was, dinnertime, early Saturday evening. The four of them were alone together in the kitchen. Maeve had to admit that the subdued atmosphere didn't suggest that it was going to be great news.

Maeve's mother was nervous. She wasn't looking any of them in the eye. She kept piling pieces of chicken up on Sam's plate, even when he said that he had plenty. And she poured chocolate milk in Maeve's dad's wineglass! She had this faraway expression on her face, and she wasn't even listening to Sam. That wasn't like her—Maeve's mom always paid attention when they talked.

"Ross," she said, looking at Maeve's father.

Maeve followed her gaze. What was wrong with her father? He looked pale, and he hadn't eaten a single bite of his dinner.

"Go ahead," he said quietly. It sounded like they'd rehearsed this.

Maeve's mom put her fork down. "Listen, you two," she said. Both Maeve and Sam looked at her intently. "Your dad and I need to talk to you about something. We know this is going to be hard for you two to hear, but ..." Her voice trailed off.

Maeve's mouth felt dry. *What was it?*

Sam gazed at his mother, his eyes fixed on hers. "Are you sick or something?" he demanded. "You look kinda funny, Mom."

Maeve's mother shook her head. "No. I'm fine, Sam." She took a deep breath. "You know, parents can have problems, too. Just like kids. And Dad and I—" She looked across the table at Maeve's father. "You've probably noticed that there's been a lot of tension between Dad and me lately. We're not entirely sure why. But lately, all we seem to do is argue. We still love each other," she added quickly. "But things have changed—we love each other in a different way now. So even though we're always going to be very close friends, we think we need some time apart. That's why ..."

Her voice trailed off and she didn't say anything. Maeve felt like her ears were burning. This was the last thing in the world she'd expected to hear. Everyone said she had the *perfect* family. Okay, her parents had arguments. They'd always had—for as long as she could remember. So maybe they'd been worse lately. Maeve's stomach churned. They'd been arguing a lot about HER, to be honest. About her bad grades. About her organizational problems. Even about the blanket project. She knew they'd been getting upset with each other ... but arguing—that wasn't the end of the world, was it? Didn't all parents do that? Couldn't they just make up, the way they always had?

Maeve wasn't sure she wanted to hear any more. "I'm

not very hungry," she said, pushing her plate away. She half-hoped that this would put an end to the discussion right away.

But her mother kept going. "Maeve, Sam. Your father and I think that it makes sense for us to separate," she said finally.

"For a while," Maeve's father added. His voice was calm and steady, the way it always was. He explained that this wasn't necessarily permanent. They needed some time apart, and in a month or two they would reevaluate. Sometimes parents needed time to be alone, just the way kids did when they weren't getting along. The most important thing, he added, was that they still loved Maeve and Sam—more than anything in the world. "Mom and I are going to work together as a team. We're going to try hard to make this okay for you guys."

Maeve was stunned. Her parents might just as well have just announced that they'd decided to move to Mars. She had no idea what to say.

But Sam did. "This is stupid!" he screamed, at nobody in particular. And as if for good measure, he threw his plate across the room. It bounced off the counter and crashed to the ground, shattering on the tile floor. Chicken and ketchup splattered everywhere.

Maeve started. Sam never yelled, and he never threw stuff. Certainly not plates. But surprisingly, her mother didn't even look mad.

"Oh, Sammy," she said, taking him in her arms. She had tears in her eyes. Nobody even got up to sweep the broken bits of plate.

Maeve wished she were eight, like Sam, and could throw something, too. But she wasn't. She was almost thirteen and had to act rational, even though it felt like her whole world was collapsing. Why did everything have to be so confusing?

Her mother was smoothing Sam's hair and talking in that voice she used when she was in planning mode. She sounded upset, but calmer. Maeve heard only bits and pieces. "Too much tension in the house lately" ... "need some time apart" ... "going to be better for you guys not to have so much arguing in the house."

"I don't see how it's going to be better for us," Maeve managed to gasp.

"Well, it may not be for anyone at first," her father admitted. "There's going to be a lot to get used to. But we're hoping that in the long run it'll be better. Your mom and I think we need to do this now. Remember, we're still your mom and dad, and we still love you. Even though we think we need to separate."

"What do you mean, *separate*?" Maeve demanded, suddenly realizing that this was going to have a huge impact on her and Sam. "What happens to US?"

"We talked about that," her mother said quickly, still stroking Sam's hair. She glanced across the table at Maeve's father. "Your dad's found a place in Washington Square ... it's only a little more than a mile away, and you can take the trolley ..."

Maeve felt bewildered. "You can't move out," she said, turning toward her father. She was so confused. Her dad lived here—with Sam and her. And Mom! This was home. None of this made any sense. "When?" she asked dully. "When's all of this supposed to happen?"

Her dad looked awkward. "Next weekend," he said at last. "We wanted to give you a little while to get used to the idea. But we didn't want it hanging over your heads for weeks, either. It's a big change, but making it happen sooner ... well, we thought that might be easier."

"Next—" Maeve was aghast. She hadn't dreamed this could all happen so fast. "But what about my awards ceremony?" she demanded. "THAT'S next weekend! You can't split up now! Not when I've actually been nominated for something!"

Her parents looked at each other. "We'll still come," her mother said. "We'll both be there for you, Maeve. Just like we promised."

She barely heard what her parents were saying. It appeared that she and Sam would have "schedules." They'd stay at home with Mom during the week, and every other weekend they'd spend at Dad's. But because Dad would still be running the cinema, he'd be downstairs every day after school. They'd spend every afternoon together. And that would be a big help, because their mom had decided to go back to work part-time.

"Work?" Maeve repeated blankly. Okay, she thought, just keep throwing this stuff out at us. What was coming next?

Her mother actually looked happy when she talked about this part. She'd wanted to do this for a long time. She'd always been interested in business—she loved helping to run the cinema. And there was a company in Brookline that needed a part-time office manager/bookkeeper. She'd had her second interview this afternoon, and they'd offered her the job.

"You know how much I love organizing things," she said with a sheepish smile. "I think I may actually be kind of good at this." She glanced from Maeve to Sam. "I know it's another thing for you to get used to. But it's only part-time, just twenty hours a week. And quite honestly, we need the money."

"But what about US?" Maeve wailed. She had always

relied on her mom to help her keep her schedule straight. Now, she was going to need that more than ever. How was she going to remember what was where? What if she left her homework over at her dad's place? Or her day planner? It was hard enough keeping her life straight right now, let alone with two separate houses to live in! Who was going to keep track of that kind of thing for her now? What about all her stuff—her homework and her clothes and her music and her guinea pigs?

"Maeve," her father said softly, leaning across the table and putting his hand over hers. "We need you to be strong. I know this isn't easy. But, we really need you to help us out. We really do think it's for the best."

"Okay," Maeve whispered. She couldn't say no when her dad asked her for something this important. But being mature had never been harder.

"Let's just leave all of this," her mom said, looking around her at the kitchen, which was now decorated with ketchup from Sam's war with his dinner plate. "Sammy, let's go read a story."

Maeve stared at her in amazement. Since when did her mother walk away from the table without clearing it and washing every last dish?

Wow, she thought. *Things really ARE changing around here.*

"Maeve," her dad said quietly, "should we surprise your mom and clean up the kitchen?"

Maeve paused. Well, at least it would give them something to do. "Okay," she said.

She got out the dustpan and helped her father sweep up the broken dish. *If only the rest of life could be fixed this easily,* she thought.

It was strangely comforting, doing something concrete

with her father. But Maeve could feel a lump forming in her throat. Why did everything have to change? Why couldn't her mother and father work out whatever was wrong between them? She didn't understand. She just knew that she wanted her father to stay. And for life to go on the way it always had.

To Tell or Not to Tell?

Maeve closed the door to her bedroom and looked around, trying to blink back tears. It was so weird—everything looked just the same as it always had. Her beloved bed with its ruffled canopy. Her bulletin board crowded with pictures of her friends—a snapshot of her friend Charlotte and her father in snorkeling gear near the Great Barrier Reef in Australia; Katani in a fabulous one-shoulder dress that she'd designed and sewn herself; Avery, arms in the air in exaltation, having just scored the winning goal against Cambridge in last year's soccer play-offs; Isabel, hard at work on a box she was mod-podging with wonderful materials taken from magazines and newspapers.

Across the room, Romeo and Juliet were swooping around in their cage, looking like nothing whatsoever was the matter. Over their cage hung Maeve's favorite poster—Orlando Bloom, shot on location in New Zealand, his hair half-falling over one eye. He was one of Maeve's heroes, ever since she'd found out that he had dyslexia, too.

Maeve opened up her laptop on her desk and connected to the Internet. Her mind was swimming. She wanted to I.M. Charlotte. Charlotte would be an amazing friend to pour her heart out to. After all, Charlotte had gone through some pretty big stuff herself.

Her mother dying when she was little ... moving around so much with her dad ... never feeling as if she fit in ...

But something made Maeve hesitate before she clicked on Charlotte's screen name in her buddy list. She didn't feel ready to face Charlotte's loving concern.

Anyway, Charlotte was in New York with her dad. She wouldn't be online.

What about Avery? Her parents were divorced. Avery didn't talk about it all that much—it had happened when she was pretty little. But she was such an upbeat, common-sense kind of person. She'd have great advice—Maeve was sure of that.

She scrolled down to Avery's screen name: 4kicks. But she didn't click on it.

She just wasn't ready for Avery's blunt, deal-with-it kind of approach. Not tonight.

What about Katani? Kgirl. Suddenly she felt her friend's calm, reasonable, wise approach to life flooding through her. Katani always seemed to have the right perspective on difficult issues. She was intelligent and level-headed. She'd be sure to have some wise words to comfort Maeve.

But somehow ... Katani could be a little reserved ... what if she held back, or felt uncomfortable about Maeve's news?

And Katani was away, too, visiting her sister at college.

Already Maeve was scrolling down to Isabel's screen name: lafrida, her newest friend, totally warm and generous. Hadn't Isabel confided in Maeve her worries about her mother's illness and treatment? She was a great listener, and offered a wonderful shoulder to cry on. She'd be sure to understand.

But Isabel thinks my mom and dad are *perfect*, Maeve thought. She said so—that afternoon we were coming back from the Sox game. Maeve didn't want her to know how far THAT was from the truth.

In fact, Maeve didn't want ANY of them to know. Suddenly she realized something. She felt really weird about her parents' news. It was EMBARRASSING to have her parents separating. Parents weren't supposed to do things like this! They were supposed to take care of you—help you with problems, listen when you needed them, drive you places, and be there for you for the ups and downs. They weren't supposed to have problems, not huge, serious ones, anyway. Hers—well, her friends thought her parents were perfect. What were they going to think now?

Maeve bit her lip. Well, she wasn't going to tell them. She wasn't going to tell ANYONE. It would be so much better, keeping it all to herself. That way she could just pretend like life was still the way it always was. Normal. Maybe that was the best way of handling this. And her parents did say that this might only be temporary.

Her friends didn't have to find out. After all, this was really about her parents. Maeve could handle it—all by herself.

Avery was pacing around the kitchen, tugging at her soccer sock. Sunday morning. Thank heavens, her mother was sleeping late this morning. She'd been out fairly late the night before at a dinner—a reunion for her graduating class from Talbot Academy.

What a weekend. Avery couldn't believe that it had only been thirty-six hours with Marty. It already felt like forever!

No sooner had Avery and her friends gotten Marty settled on Friday evening than her mother had come home. She was in a great mood, full of energy and plans. She couldn't wait for her Talbot reunion.

"Avery, I haven't seen these old friends of mine for years. It's just so nice catching up with them and finding out what they've been up to." Avery had heard people describe her mother as a "people person" and she knew what they meant. Elizabeth Madden—she was called "Bif" for short—collected friends the way some people collect pottery or CDs. She was unbelievably friendly—Avery was always dying of embarrassment, listening to her mom go on and on when she met people—even people at the grocery store! She had a huge heart and she loved hearing other people's stories. The most embarrassing was when she talked about Avery right in front of her.

"I can't help being proud of you," her mother always said, leaning over to tweak her daughter's ponytail. Avery grimaced. She didn't know how to tactfully let her mother know that she hated it when her mother bragged about her. "She's on the premier-level soccer team!" her mother would say—even before anyone asked. Ouch! Sure, it was nice her mom was proud of her. But couldn't she be SILENT about it?

"I promised Sally Henderson that I'd find our old yearbooks so we could look at them tomorrow night at dinner," her mother was saying as she came into the house on Friday night. "Avery, would you help me tomorrow morning? I know they're up in the loft of the carriage house, but I'm not sure where. Do you have time before soccer practice to help me look for them?"

Avery gulped. The loft? Of the carriage house?

Her mother hadn't been in the carriage house in ages. Why did she suddenly have to go rummaging around up there looking for old yearbooks? Of all the bad luck in the world. What was Avery supposed to do about Marty?

Well, that was crisis number one. Avery had to use all her ingenuity on that one. The only thing she could think of was to wait until her mom was in bed—and that wasn't until almost eleven o'clock!—and then sneak out to the carriage house and grab Marty. AND all of his stuff. It took three separate trips. She couldn't think where to hide him, but she finally decided that the laundry room was the best idea. At least it was warm down there, and her mother never did laundry on the weekends.

But Marty did not like being transplanted in the least. He kept cocking his head and looking pleadingly at her, as if he were saying, "*Stay with me.*" If only she could. She hated leaving Marty alone.

Saturday morning, Avery overslept. Who could help it? She'd been up 'til midnight trying to calm Marty down and keep him quiet. She could hear him whimpering through the heating vents. What if her mother had heard, too?

But on Saturday morning her mother seemed focused on yearbooks. "Come help me, Avery," she said enthusiastically, throwing open the door and letting the sunlight stream in. "I'm dying to find those yearbooks. Let's go hunt for them!"

Avery rubbed the sleep out of her eyes. Yawning, she

threw on a pair of sweats and followed her mother downstairs. They were just at the back door when she heard it—a definite, distinct yelp.

Marty. Wanting to go out.

Avery's mother turned and looked at her. "What was that?" she demanded.

"Ohh—that was me. Sorry. I just kind of ... squeaked a little. It was a yawn that turned into a sneeze," Avery improvised. She grabbed her jacket. "Come on, let's go find those yearbooks!"

Her mother frowned, looking down at the heat vent. "Are you sure that was you, Avery? 'Cause I could have sworn—"

"Seriously, Mom. I'm gonna be late for soccer if we don't get going," Avery said.

Five minutes later she was making her way up the ladder at the back of the carriage house, flashlight in hand. "Mom, what on earth have you GOT up here?" she cried. The loft of the carriage house was filled with cobwebs and boxes ... and stacks of books.

"You're going to have to come up and look. I don't know where to begin," she added.

"There's a big box marked TALBOT ACADEMY," her mother called up to her. Then her voice changed expression. "Avery, what's this?" she demanded.

Avery turned around and peered back down at her.

Shoot. Her mother was holding up Marty's leash. It must've fallen down the night before when she was making her last trip with Marty's blankets and food bowl.

"Uh ... I ... uh, I don't know," Avery stammered. Brilliant. "I think it's a leash," she added lamely.

"I can see that. But what's it DOING here?" her mother asked.

Avery didn't answer.

Her mother rubbed her eyes with a frown on her face. "Avery," she said suddenly, "I feel a little itchy."

"It must be the dust," Avery said helpfully. "It's really dusty in here, Mom. You shouldn't be in here."

Meanwhile her mind was racing. It wasn't going to take her mother long to put two and two together. The leash ... the yelping sounds coming from the basement ...

Fortunately, her mother's cell phone had rung. It was Sally, eager to make plans to meet before the dinner.

"Saved by the bell," was the way Avery explained it on Sunday to Isabel and Maeve.

"But this afternoon she's having a whole bunch of Talbot people over for tea to plan the event. What am I going to do with Marty? He keeps making *noises* down there," Avery cried.

"We'll have to smuggle him out somehow," Isabel said. "Maybe Maeve and I can take him to the park this afternoon until Charlotte gets back."

"Yeah! Let's just take him back to your house, Maeve," Avery suggested.

"I can't!" Maeve said quickly. When Isabel and Avery looked quizzically at her she added, "I mean ... it just wouldn't work out today." How could she let her friends come over? Her dad was busy packing up boxes right in the middle of the living room!

"Maeve, things can't be worse at your place than mine," Avery said.

If you only knew, Maeve thought miserably. But she didn't tell Avery. "Okay," she said at last, trying to figure out a solution while she talked. "I can just take him to the park, I guess ... or keep him outside and away from Sam until Charlotte gets back."

The three girls huddled up in Avery's room, trying to make a plan. Finally they agreed that the best thing to do would be to smuggle Marty out in Avery's soccer bag and take him to the park. All they had to do was to get past Avery's mother. And that wasn't going to be easy.

"Does she always talk on the phone for so long?" Isabel demanded, peering down over the banister.

"She *loves* the phone," Avery admitted. "She's worse than my brother, and that's saying a lot. My mom is the friendliest woman in all of Brookline. I just wish she weren't quite so friendly right now. I wish she could kind of hole up in her study for an hour or so and let us make a quick Marty getaway."

"Avery!"

"Good—she's off now," Avery whispered.

Avery's mother came up the stairs, beaming when she saw Isabel and Maeve. "Hi girls!" She gave them a quick wave. "Did Avery tell you about the reunion tea I'm having today? Would you girls like to stick around and help out?"

"They can't," Avery said abruptly. "I mean—sorry, Mom, but they're SO busy. They have to go to the library and work on the Heritage Museum project."

"Tea sounds so nice," Isabel began, but Avery nudged her in the ribs.

"Avery, I'm trying to find that peach-colored blouse of mine. Have you seen it?" her mother asked. "I've looked everywhere. I thought Carla might have put it in your closet." Carla was the Maddens' housekeeper. "Oh, I know! It must be down in the laundry." She rubbed her eyes. "That's funny ... I thought the ragweed season was over. My eyes feel a little itchy."

Avery panicked. She jumped up, grabbing her mother by the arm. "NO!" she shrieked. "I mean, don't wear that peach blouse. That looks so ... um ..." She looked helplessly at her friends. Avery didn't know enough about clothes to come up with the right description here. She needed help.

"It's just the wrong color," Maeve broke in quickly.

"Avery," her mother said, staring at her. "Since when are you so interested in what I wear? You've never cared before about clothes." She was about to say something else, but a big sneeze overpowered her.

"Bless you," Isabel said promptly.

"I just want you to look good, that's all," Avery said. "You know that really fuzzy sweater of yours? That blue one? That would look awesome with what you're wearing."

Her mother looked amazed. "You really think so, Avery?" She inspected her navy blue slacks, puzzled. "Well, maybe you're right. Okay. I'll go get it." She seemed a little pleased that Avery was suddenly so interested in what she was wearing—clearly a first.

"Phew," Avery said, when her mother was out of the room. "That was SO close."

She shut the door behind her, turning to face Isabel and Maeve.

"Okay. We better get Marty out of here. NOW." Avery sounded desperate.

Smuggling Marty out of the laundry room proved to be harder than it seemed. Avery's mother was opening up the door for the first of her guests, her laughter bubbling up as the girls crept down to the laundry room. Her laughter ... and several very loud sneezes.

"I knew this wasn't a good idea, Avery. It really isn't fair to your mom," said Maeve.

Avery looked down at her shoes. "I know. I feel really awful. It's just that I so wanted to have Marty with me for a little while. I just didn't think it through. I thought I could protect my mother and have Marty too. Just my luck. She never goes in that carriage house."

"Well," said Isabel. "You probably should have just told her from the beginning."

"Yeah, you should have, Ave."

Suddenly, Scott stood right in front of them, Marty in his arms. The little guy was overjoyed to see all the girls. He squirmed vigorously in Scott's arms, obviously wanting to get to his girls. "Settle down, little dude," Scott said sternly to Marty, who cocked his head and suddenly became very still.

Maeve, Isabel, and Avery stared at Scott nervously. They all felt a little intimidated. Avery spoke up first.

"I know, Scott. I made a big mistake and now Mom is sneezing and we just want to get Marty out as soon as possible. I don't want Mom to have a full-blown allergy attack."

Then she asked sheepishly, "Will you help us?"

"Help you? Mmm ... let's see ..."

Exasperated, Avery snapped at him. "Come on Scott, please. I do stuff for you all the time."

Scott took a deep breath which seemed to the girls to last a lifetime. "Okay," he finally said with a smile. Give me the bag with the dog and I'll meet you guys in the park."

"SSSHhh," Avery said, holding open the soccer bag. "Hop in, little guy."

But Marty didn't want to go anywhere. He sat back on his haunches, panting happily, his bright eyes moving from one girl to the next.

"Marty, COME ON. We've got to go," Avery said pleadingly.

Marty consented to crawl into the soccer bag after Maeve threw in a doggie chew. But the minute he was inside he started barking.

"Okay, you guys go upstairs and try to keep Mom and her friend distracted. I'll sneak him out the back door," Scott said.

The girls were halfway up the stairs when they heard Avery's mother's voice. "It's so strange," she was saying to her friend. "I seem to be getting a little bit of a rash. I have no idea what can be causing this! It's almost as if—"

She came out into the hallway, her glance falling on the wriggling soccer bag. "Scott, what have you got in that bag?" Isabel and Maeve, their expressions a mixture of embarrassment and fear, didn't know what to do. Avery's mother was rubbing both of her arms, looking back and forth from Avery and Scott to the wiggling soccer bag. Suddenly Scott leaned in and gave his mother a kiss. "Gotta go, Mom. I'll catch you later," and he bolted out the door.

"What is going on here Avery? Was there a dog in that bag? AVERY," her mother said loudly. "What are you all up to?" A sneeze shook her whole body.

"Ooops! We've got to run, too," Avery said, running after Scott, with Maeve and Isabel hurrying after her.

"Avery Koh Madden," Mrs. Madden said suddenly, "I think you and I better have a talk later—" Another sneeze came.

It looked like her four-legged friend had already overstayed his welcome.

BLUE DAY

"Hey!" Maeve's father said, coming out onto the stoop to sit beside her.

It was late Sunday afternoon and Maeve was keeping Marty company, waiting for Charlotte and her dad to come by and pick him up. Maeve had called Charlotte, who was at the airport, and told her the whole story. They'd be by in half an hour to collect Marty, but for now Maeve wanted to keep him outside. Sam had been through enough in the past twenty-four hours—he didn't need to be scared about having a dog around.

"You doing okay?" her dad asked her softly, leaning over to give Marty a quick pat.

Maeve nodded. "I guess," she said.

There were so many things she wanted to ask her dad, but saying anything at all right now seemed all wrong. She couldn't beg him to change his mind. He'd made her promise to try to be "mature." Maeve felt helpless—and confused.

"Listen," he said slowly. "You were saying something yesterday about wanting to talk to me about what it was like when I was growing up. I never told you much about this, but when I was about your age, my dad lost his job. It was really hard on our family. He didn't find work again for almost three years. I was really embarrassed—I didn't want the other kids to know that he was unemployed."

Maeve felt her eyes sting with tears. Had he read her mind somehow? How could her father know her so well?

"Finally, he got a job," her father continued. "He got trained and started working as a plumber. Everyone else I knew ... their dads were doctors and lawyers. But Dad used to let me and my friends play with all his pipes and tools, and he was really patient. He taught us how to fix everything. All my friends thought that was really great." Maeve smiled. She could just imagine her father and grandfather laughing while they fixed the toilet!

Maeve fiddled with Marty's leash. "And then Grandpa started his own company, right?" she asked.

Her father grinned. "Owned his own company after about five years. Then he sold it and bought the home renovation business that he ran until he retired. I was proud of him, Maeve. He kept his head held high, even when he was out of work. He always told me that the most important thing you have is your own sense of self-worth. That, and honesty. Those were the two things he cared about more than anything."

Maeve wound Marty's leash around and around her finger. "I wish you and Mom could stay together," she whispered.

"I know you do, Maeve. And you know what? I wish that too. But for now, you've got to believe me. It's the right thing for us right now. Kids can face big challenges and come out just fine."

Maeve wasn't so sure. She couldn't imagine getting through a single day without her dad around. How was she going to manage once he'd moved out?

"Do you know what the word 'resilience' means?" her father asked her.

Maeve shook her head. "You know me, Dad. I'm not so good with big words," she said truthfully.

"Well—it means being strong, even in hard times. Being able to roll with the punches. Maeve, I know that you have this quality. So does Sam, but he doesn't know it yet." Her father leaned over to give her a hug. "You're going to find out that you're more resilient than you knew. That doesn't mean that you won't get sad, or feel upset about this. But it does mean that you're going to be okay in the long run. Just trust yourself, and trust me because I love you ... okay?"

Maeve nodded. Her throat ached with tears, and she had to concentrate furiously on Marty not to break down then and there.

7

Teaming Up

Maeve woke up early on Monday morning—even before her pink guinea pig alarm clock made its usual buzzing sound. For a moment, she couldn't remember what was different. Then it all came rushing back.

She was dressed and ready for school in record time. Not only that, but Maeve was the first one in the kitchen. No sign of her mom or dad. Unheard of. Breakfast wasn't ready yet—usually her mom set the table the night before, but not today. Maeve decided to pitch in. She put out her brother's Star Wars bowl and his goofy marshmallow cereal, and she tried not to be negative as she poured the cereal out for him—although how he could eat so much green in the morning was beyond her.

Maeve's mom came in, still in her bathrobe. Her hair was half wet and half dry, and she was wearing stockings and high heels under her robe. She seemed like she was in a panic. "Oh my gosh, Maeve, thanks so much!" she cried when she saw Maeve setting the table. "I'm just not used to getting myself ready in the morning! I couldn't even find a blow-dryer. I borrowed yours." She started dashing madly around the kitchen, talking as she went. "Today's my first day of work," she added, pulling out the orange juice. "I think I'm a little nervous ... I just hope I make an okay impression," she went on, sounding almost shy.

There were a million things Maeve wanted to ask her, but nothing felt right. Instead, what came out sounded a little silly. "What are you going to wear?"

Her mother's face relaxed into a relieved smile. "I was kind of wondering that myself," she admitted. "I guess I'd better not wear my carpool outfit."

Maeve laughed. Her mother's carpool outfit was pretty awful. Running tights, a sweatshirt, and clogs. "You'd better not," she agreed. "D'you want some help, Mom? I'm pretty good as a fashion consultant."

In the few minutes before Sam came storming into the kitchen, Maeve helped her mother rummage through her closet. Wow, Maeve thought. Her mom hadn't bought herself anything new to wear in ages. Maeve felt a sudden twinge of guilt. Her mom always shopped for Maeve, come to think of it, whenever there was extra money. She sure hadn't spent much on herself.

"How about this?" Maeve said at last, taking out a gray skirt and a navy sweater. It was pretty simple, but it looked elegant. "You could put a jacket over this. It looks nice and office-y."

Maeve's mother took the skirt and sweater, not even looking at them. She was looking at Maeve instead, her eyes misting over. "Thanks," she said softly. She acted like Maeve had just done something huge to help her.

It felt strangely good to help her mother for a change, instead of being the flaky, disorganized daughter who always needed to be rescheduled. "Good luck today, Mom," Maeve said. And then on impulse, she gave her a hug. She had to make it a quick one, and then bolted out of the room. Otherwise, they'd both be bawling!

ભ

"Did she figure it out?" Isabel demanded. "Did your mom guess it was Marty who was giving her hives?"

The girls were at their lockers early Monday morning— all but Maeve, who wasn't at school yet. Avery, Katani, Isabel, and Charlotte were filling each other in on the weekend. Marty was safely back where he belonged, enjoying the Statue-of-Liberty-shaped dog biscuits Charlotte had brought him back ... and all the extra attention, too.

Charlotte and Katani had heard all about Marty's getaway and Avery's near miss. Now they wanted to know if Avery's mother had figured out that she'd had an extra houseguest for the weekend.

"She knows," Avery said glumly. "She started to grill me, but thank heavens, those friends of hers all showed up for tea, so she couldn't keep asking questions.

"It's so sad," Avery continued, opening her locker with one quick spin of the combination. "Last night I dreamed that my mom stopped being allergic to dogs and she let me bring Marty home with me, and he got to sleep right on the end of my bed!" She shook her head, her dark hair falling across her face as she pushed it back impatiently. "Only when I woke up it turned out that what I thought was Marty was really only my skateboard."

"You sleep with your skateboard?" Isabel asked, shaking her head. "That's dedication." She frowned. "Or weirdness— I can't tell which."

"I NEED a dog," Avery moaned. "Why on earth did I get stuck with an allergic mother when I am totally, one-hundred percent a dog person? How fair is that?"

Isabel laughed, but Charlotte gave Avery a sympathetic smile. She knew that Avery was serious. She really adored dogs, and Charlotte had a feeling that this longing of hers wasn't going to go away.

"What's wrong with Walter?" Katani asked in her "I really don't like reptiles" voice. To Katani, Walter wasn't much better than a deadly germ. He'd slithered around Avery's room one night when Katani was sleeping over and she'd almost had a heart attack. "That thing better look out," she'd cried, "or he's going to get turned into a pair of shoes before he knows what hit him!"

"Walter," Avery said sorrowfully, "is wonderful—for a snake. But I feel like I need something ... you know, a little cuddlier and a lot more interactive." She shook her head again. "I just have to figure out some way to help my mother get unallergic so she can change her mind. But I don't know how!"

"You should really tell your mom how much you want a dog. She's so nice I bet she will listen to you," Charlotte said. "If she knew how badly you want a dog, she might even get those new shots that are supposed to help your allergies. I've heard those can really work for some people."

"Hey," Katani said, pulling her notebook out of her locker. "Anyone seen Maeve? She was supposed to meet me at the corner this morning, but she wasn't there."

Isabel and Charlotte both shook their heads. "I usually see her on my way to school," Charlotte said, "but I didn't today."

Avery shrugged. "She probably slept late. Come on, guys. Ms. Rodriguez wants us to fill her in on our Heritage Museum stuff this morning—we'd better not be late."

CR

One thing Maeve loved about Ms. Rodriguez was that she always started off slowly on Monday mornings, asking about their weekends. She wasn't one of those teachers who seemed to think kids only existed when they were at school.

"So," she said with a smile. "How was the weekend?"

The mere mention of the word "weekend" produced excited whispering from Anna and Joline, but fortunately a couple of other kids raised their hands to fill Ms. Rodriguez in on what they'd done. Pete, Dillon, and Nick had gone to a Patriots game. Riley's band was practicing a new song, getting ready for a Battle of the Bands contest coming up later in the fall. Sammy Andropovitch had gone hiking with his family. Samantha Simmons, who loved dropping hints about how rich her family was, had been down to the Cape, "winterizing" their summer house—whatever that meant!

Maeve kept her eyes averted. Don't call on me. *Please, don't call on me.* She needn't have worried. Ms. Rodriguez almost never put kids on the spot.

Maeve sure wasn't going to volunteer anything about HER weekend. She could just imagine the looks on everyone's faces if she raised her hand and said casually, "Oh, my mom and dad are going to separate. And my dad's moving out this weekend ..."

Her face turned red just thinking about it.

Yikes. It was going to take a real effort to make sure nobody found out.

Charlotte raised her hand. "I went to New York City with my dad. It was great—we took the ferry out to Ellis Island and to the Statue of Liberty. I'd never been there before," she said.

Ms. Rodriguez beamed. "Ellis Island," she repeated. She explained to the class that for those who didn't know, this was the place where immigrants to the United States had arrived by the tens of thousands in the late nineteenth and early twentieth centuries. "Did you actually go into the building?"

Charlotte nodded. "It turns out you can find out about family members who came through there," she said. "We found out some information about my father's grandfather, Jonathan Ramsey. He came over from England in the 1890s."

Ms. Rodriguez looked delighted. "What a perfect transition, Charlotte. This leads right into what I wanted to talk with all of you about this morning. As you know, Ms. O'Reilly and I are teaming up so that you can work on your Heritage Museum projects in English for the next several weeks, as well as in social studies. I'll be helping each of you come up with interview questions to use when you talk to older relatives. Also, I'll be helping you to write your reports. I'm sure you learned some interesting things about your great-grandfather that will be useful for this project, Charlotte." She looked expectantly around the room. "So this afternoon during English class, get ready to do some brainstorming. Think hard about what you want to learn and about the questions that will help you to find those answers."

Maeve bit her lip. *Questions*, she thought. *What I want to know.*

She fiddled with her keyboard.

What I Want To Know:
1. Do people's histories drive them
   apart? Do my mom and dad argue because
   they come from different backgrounds?
2. Am I going to end up getting divorced
   if my mom and dad do?
3. What does it mean if you still love
   each other but want to live in
   different places? How does THAT make
   sense?
4. How can you love someone one way and
   then it changes? I don't get that.
5. Is arguing always bad? Why does it
   happen?

Maeve knew that these weren't the questions she was supposed to be coming up with. But right now, they were the ones that were on her mind.

ର

The Abigail Adams lunchroom was crowded, as usual. Kids were jostling each other in the lunch line, hurrying to grab seats at their favorite tables, or crowding around the drink machine at one end of the cafeteria. Maeve saw Katani and Avery waving to her from across the room at their usual table. She didn't have much of an appetite, but she headed over to sit with them anyway.

"Maeve, come join us!" Katani said, gesturing at the chair next to her. "Isabel and Charlotte are still in the lunch line." She wrinkled her nose. "It's the Abigail Adams attempt at mac and cheese today. Not exactly my favorite."

"Carbs in a bowl. That's what I call it," Avery muttered.

Maeve shook her head, hoping that she didn't look as bad as she felt. She kept thinking that it must be written all over her face: "PARENTS SEPARATING! Pity this girl!" At least she remembered how to spell "Separating." Her mother had taught her years ago that you could always remember how to spell it because there was "a rat" in the middle of the word. How strange that she would think of that now.

She'd been feeling out of it all morning. She kept wondering how her mother's first day of work was going. And what about her dad? Was he packing boxes? What would it be like tonight at dinner? Would they all just eat together, like everything was still normal? Would they get to hear about his new place? So many changes ... and all so fast.

It was so hard to believe this was all really going to happen.

But maybe, Maeve thought suddenly, it didn't have to. Maybe just TALKING about separating would be enough to shock her parents back into realizing how much they needed each other. If she and Sam were super-helpful and on their VERY best behavior, there wouldn't be so much tension in the house. Maybe her parents would see how much calmer and saner life could be.

Maeve thought she could start right away. She could offer to help make dinner tonight. She could get every bit of homework done without even being reminded. She could even straighten up her room.

After all, Maeve thought, her parents said that they still loved each other. And they seemed like they were looking out for each other's feelings now more than they had in ages. Hadn't her father wanted to clean up the kitchen for her mom on Saturday night? And her dad had told her last night that her mom had helped him find his new apartment. In the movies, people changed their minds and decided to stay together. Why couldn't it happen like that in real life, too?

"Maeve? Are you okay?" Katani said, putting her hand on Maeve's arm and looking at her friend with concern. "We've been talking for the past few minutes and you didn't even hear us!"

"Oh—sorry," Maeve said, sitting up and struggling to smile. "I just don't feel right," she added suddenly. "I'm ... I don't know, my stomach is kind of bugging me."

Why don't I want my friends to know about my mom and dad? she wondered. Maeve knew that sooner or later they were going to find out. Just not now, she thought. I'm just not ready yet.

Isabel and Charlotte were winding their way through the lunchroom, trying to balance their trays, and before long everyone was busy talking about the Heritage Museum. Nobody seemed to notice that Maeve was being really quiet.

"You know that loft up in our carriage house?" Avery said. "I bet there's some really cool old stuff up there that I could find. Mom says she hasn't gone through it in ages."

Katani nodded. "Going through old stuff is really cool. I talked to my grandmother this weekend on our ride up to see Candice. She thinks she may even have something dating all the way back before the Civil War in the trunk her mother left her."

"I haven't talked to my mom yet, but my Aunt Lourdes thinks we may have some things in her attic. We're going to start looking up there this week," Isabel said, her eyes shining. "I was thinking of trying to make a collage out of some old photographs. Do you think Ms. O'Reilly would like that?"

Maeve heard everyone chattering around her, but she

couldn't bring herself to join in the conversation. She knew that if she tried to talk, her voice would sound funny. And then her friends would want to know why. She wouldn't be able to keep her news to herself once they started grilling her.

"MAEVE," Avery said, staring at her. "Earth to Maeve!"

"We were just asking," Charlotte said patiently, "if you knew who you were going to interview for the Heritage Museum yet?"

"Uh—I don't know yet," Maeve mumbled. She could see it now ... her room for the Heritage Museum would be divided in half. Mom's side and Dad's side. And nothing in the whole display touching.

"Are you okay?" Katani was asking her. "You seem like you're a zillion miles away."

"Oh, I was just thinking about the thing on Friday night," Maeve fibbed. "I'm kind of nervous. You know what? ... I think I'm going to head over to the library to work on my speech. Just in case I win," she added quickly.

"During lunch?" Katani asked, still staring at her. Maeve was usually the one talking everybody else out of heading to the library.

But this, Maeve told herself, was different. She really did want to work on her speech. Who could tell? Maybe it would be the final thing that would convince her parents to stay together.

MAEVE'S ACCEPTANCE SPEECH: DRAFT 1

First of all, I really want to thank my mom and dad. They've always shown me that love and communication are the two most important things in the world. I've always felt how much they love me ... and my brother ... and most of all, each other.

The way Maeve imagined it, the crowd would roar with applause ... she'd accept the huge gold trophy that she was certain went along with the award. And her parents, sitting right in the front row, would hug each other, tears in their eyes, and swear then and there to stay together ... forever.

A perfect Hollywood ending. Now all she had to do was win the award ... and write the perfect speech.

And everything else would just fall into place.

CHAPTER
8

Somewhere Back in Time

"K now why this place is so great?" Avery asked her friends, turning from her favorite window of the Tower room—the one that looked east, toward Boston and her beloved Fenway Park. "Cause we always seem to get all our best ideas when we're up here!"

It was Tuesday afternoon, and the girls were studying up in the Tower. They all needed to work on interview questions for the Heritage Museum, and they'd convinced each other that they'd work a million times better if they were all together.

Charlotte knew exactly what Avery was talking about. The Tower room felt like another world. The girls had found it together almost by accident one night during a sleepover. From the outside, it looked like the cupola on the top of the Victorian house that the Ramseys were renting might be just decorative. But inside, the Tower room felt like a secret hideaway. It was partly the sloping floor, the wide floorboards, and the long high windows. The room was fairly small, but that just made it feel cozier. Whether they were planning an adventure or just sleeping over together in the Tower, there was always something magical about this place!

This afternoon, homework was the rule of the day. Charlotte and Katani were sharing Charlotte's writing desk. Katani was sitting in the old lime-green swivel chair, which she kept spinning around to help her concentrate. Avery, Maeve, and Isabel were sprawled out on their stomachs on the floor, their books and notebooks spread all around them. And Marty was doing his best to help, jumping around from one girl to the next and panting with excitement.

"You're so lucky, Char. I love studying with Marty," Avery said, snuggling closer to the furry little dog, who licked her face enthusiastically. Avery laughed, pulling back a little. "He's so much more fun than a skateboard!" she joked.

"It's Heritage Museum time, Avery," Katani chided her.

"Listen to what I have so far," Isabel said, clambering to her feet. "Ms. Rodriguez said that we should start by listing what we want to know, right? Well, here goes."

Things I Wonder About My Family's History

1. *What was it like a long time ago when we lived in Mexico?*
2. *Was it hard moving to America? Why did our family come here? When did we learn to speak English?*
3. *What were the biggest differences between Mexican and American life?*
4. *What was the hardest thing to get used to in America?*
5. *What member of my family am I most like?*

"That's good," Charlotte said approvingly. "I like all of it. And the last question is a great idea!" Her eyes sparkled. "Wouldn't it be amazing to find someone in your family who lived a long time ago who loves a lot of the same things that you do?"

Katani cleared her throat. "Okay, you guys. Listen to my questions so far." She hopped up off the Lime Swivel to read her list.

What I Want to Know About My Family History or Who Else Likes to Sew, Anyway?

1. *What were my great-grandparents like? I know all sorts of things about my grandmother, but I'm curious about her parents. What were they like? When did they come to Boston?*
2. *Were there any great leaders in my family? (I'm kind of hoping to find someone inspirational in my family's past!)*
3. *What kind of stuff did my family have to deal with, being African American a long time ago?*
4. *Are Grandma Ruby and I the only ones who like to sew and design things in my family?*

"Awesome," Avery said approvingly. She flicked her yo-yo expertly. "I'm still working on mine," she admitted. "What about you, Maeve?"

Maeve frowned. "Still working," she said quickly.

She was grateful when Charlotte took the spotlight off her by reading from her own list.

Charlotte's Questions (DRAFT)

1. *I know that my mother was a teacher. Were there teachers on both sides of our family? And what*

about writing? Were there writers on my mother's side of the family, too?

2. *Was anyone else in our family interested in studying the stars?*

3. *I also wonder where we came from. I love to travel, like my dad does, but I've always wanted a place to call home. I wonder if our family came from one special place, or lots of different places. I think learning about that will help me to understand my father's love of travel better.*

Maeve listened to Charlotte's quiet voice as she read out loud from her list. Suddenly, she had an almost overwhelming desire to tell her friends what was going on with her parents. She knew that they'd want to know something this big. They'd probably kill her when they found out ... IF they found out.

But it doesn't have to happen, Maeve reminded herself, packing up her book bag. If everything goes the way I hope it does, maybe there's no reason to tell them. Maybe the whole thing will blow over and I won't have to say a word.

"Hey, I've gotta go," Maeve said, slinging her bag over one shoulder. "I've got to help my parents do some stuff at home."

"But we haven't even started designing your outfit for Friday night!" Katani wailed.

"I know! But it's five o'clock already." Maeve grabbed her day planner, which had slid out of her book bag onto the floor.

"Maeve, you are so ORGANIZED these days," Katani said admiringly. "Getting nominated for that award has totally changed you. Who knows? Maybe you're really a Virgo in disguise!"

"See you guys," Maeve called as she hurried out the door, giving them all a quick wave.

If Katani only knew, she was thinking. Maeve hadn't changed one bit because of being nominated for the award. It was life at home that was changing her. And it wasn't because she was suddenly organized. It was because she was doing everything in her power to keep her mom and dad together.

CHAPTER
9

Even Model Daughters Oversleep

Maeve opened one eye. Her alarm clock was buzzing away. Darn! Seven thirty! Had she managed to push the snooze button AGAIN? Why hadn't her mom come and woken her up, the way she always did when Maeve overslept?

Maeve jumped out of bed like a three-alarm fire was raging through the house. She grabbed her favorite blue jeans and a T-shirt from the pile on her chair. Yuck—there was a chocolate stain on the shirt. Everything she owned seemed to be dirty or in the wash. Where were the neatly laundered clothes her mother always left stacked just inside her door, waiting for Maeve to put them away?

This going-back-to-work business had its downside. It was nice that Maeve's mom was so excited about her new job. But still, a girl had her limits. After a scramble, she finally found something half decent to wear. Maeve grabbed

❁ 85 ❁

her laptop and her book bag, ignoring the plaintive looks on Romeo's and Juliet's furry little faces. "No time to play, guys. I am late, late, late," Maeve sang out, racing down the hall. Her stomach was growling. Breakfast ... she was definitely in need of one of her mom's famous power breakfasts. Maeve liked to moan and groan when her mother made Sam and her eat what she liked to call "real food" for breakfast, but today, the thought made Maeve smile. She was famished. Scrambled eggs and buttered toast would be just the thing to get her energy level up before school.

But when Maeve dashed into the kitchen, it was completely quiet. No sign of her mother anywhere, and instead of a delicious, piping hot breakfast, there was a note on the kitchen table.

"Maeve, be a love and get Sam some cereal before school. My boss asked me to come in early today, and Dad has a fund-raiser breakfast downtown. Lots of love, Mom."

Maeve stared at the note. GREAT. It was hard work trying to be a model daughter. Especially a model daughter who was running thirty minutes behind.

The kitchen door cracked open. Sam looked like a wreck. Worse than usual, Maeve thought, noticing that half of his hair was sticking up on one side and he was still wearing his pajama top. Great. So no hot breakfast, and now she was supposed to magically get herself ready for school and get Sam ready for the bus. This was just GREAT. Maeve was getting sick of model daughter behavior. She wouldn't mind just being herself again, to tell the truth.

"Where's Mom?" Sam demanded, his lower lip wobbling.

Maeve was about to snap that she wanted to know the exact same thing, but something in her little brother's expression made her stop short. "Oh—she had to go to work early today," she said, trying to sound like she had it all under control. She banged open a few cupboards, looking around for Sam's favorite cup. What kind of eight-year-old, she thought to herself, is such a major brainiac that he can tell you every single battle that ever happened in the Civil War, but still likes to drink his juice out of a Star Wars cup?

"Here!" she said triumphantly, banging the cup on the table. She banged it too hard, though, and Sam jumped.

That was just enough to get Sam to cry. Little tears leaking out of the corners of his eyes, and he just stood there, looking completely tragic. It made Maeve's heart break.

"Don't worry," she said, gulping. "It's fine, Sam. She just had to go in early today. I'm sure it won't usually be like this. I'll make you breakfast, okay? Just—just don't cry like that!"

"I hate this," Sam shouted.

Maeve stared at him. Poor kid. This was hard for Maeve, but it was obviously really hard for Sam, too. She hadn't really thought that much about what he must be feeling.

Maeve took a step closer to him. She closed her eyes, took a deep breath, and—*well, here goes nothing,* she thought as put her arms around him. He didn't actually feel that gruesome—and he didn't even smell bad. Considering.

"It's going to be okay," she whispered. "I promise."

She held him for a little while, and he seemed to calm down. The strange thing was, Maeve felt a little better, too. She didn't even scream when he sniffled right onto her one clean T-shirt. She made him cinnamon toast and found him his green marshmallow cereal. Actually, the cinnamon toast was good—just as good as Mom's. Maeve ended up eating three pieces. By the time breakfast was done she was feeling much better.

"Come on," she said to Sam when they were done eating. "I'll take you to the bus on my way to school."

The house was empty as she closed the door behind them. No Mom to call out after them, wishing them a good day. No Mom urging Maeve to hurry, reminding her to brush her teeth after breakfast (she forgot!) or asking if she had her homework.

Her homework! Shoot! She'd left her completed math assignment on the dining room table, right where she and Matt had worked on it last night!

Maeve spun around. "Sam, we have to go back."

"Why?" he demanded, wiping his nose on his sleeve. YUCK.

"I forgot something," she told him, passing him a tissue.

She ran back into the apartment and grabbed her homework, stuffing it into her bag with a sudden feeling of ... what was it? Pride? Satisfaction?

It felt good taking charge of this stuff on her own. Maeve hoped her mom wasn't going to make a habit of these early morning work hours. But at the same time, she was kind of proud of herself for being able to take care of Sam. Not to mention herself.

10

What Holds Together

Charlotte's Journal

I know I haven't written in ages. I'm up on my balcony, with Marty ... and my big quilt wrapped around both of us. The nights are definitely getting colder—not sure how much longer I'm going to be able to sneak out here and look for stars.

It's so funny about constellations. When you know the pattern that you're looking for, you can usually find it. But if you don't know what shape to look for, you can sometimes see your own shapes up in the sky. I love trying to find my own shapes up there. An Eiffel Tower ... a Tower. But when it comes to real constellations, my favorite is Orion. Dad's the one who taught me that you can see Orion in both hemispheres. When we were in the Serengeti that used to make me feel less far away from everything else I knew ...

So I asked Dad tonight at dinner about what it was like for him when he was growing up. And guess what?

Dad NEVER got to travel when he was little. He told me that his parents lived outside of Chicago and they didn't really like to travel very much. Dad was so curious about the rest of the world, he used to get out all of these huge travel books from the library and pore over them, dreaming of all the places he wanted to go to one day. He always swore that when he grew up, he was going to live differently. And then he met Mom, and she felt the same way that he did. They both had this saying: "A home should be a ship, and not an anchor." They wanted to spend their whole lives traveling around the world ... and after I was born, they started to do that. When Mom died, Dad wanted to carry on with their dream. I did love hearing my dad's stories. It helps me to understand him so much more.

I asked Dad tonight if I could interview my grand-father and learn more about what it was like for him, growing up. He said, "Of course."

℞

Maeve, Katani, and Isabel met at the front entrance of Abigail Adams after school on Wednesday.

"Don't even try to get away from us. This is an ambush. It's time for the *Kgirl* Award Ceremony Makeover!" Katani said gleefully, taking Maeve by the arm. "And don't you dare try to wriggle your way out of this! I don't want to hear a word about homework or the Heritage Museum or anything else!"

"You have an awards ceremony to get ready for," Isabel added. The girls each grabbed one of Maeve's arms and pretended to march her up the street.

"I don't have any money, you guys. Honestly," Maeve protested.

"Who said anything about money? It's time for Maeve's

home shopping network," Katani sang out happily. "We're going straight to your closet to see what you've got. And then it's time to put the Designing Duo to work."

Maeve thought fast. Her mom would be at home, and probably Sam, too. But her mom wouldn't say anything personal in front of her friends—she could count on that. Or at least she hoped that she could. And Katani and Isabel were right. She DID need something to wear on Friday.

"Okay," she said, relenting. "But I don't have very long. I have—"

"Homework," Isabel and Katani said in unison, winking at each other.

Maeve's cheeks flushed. Clearly her "model daughter" behavior had not gone unnoticed among her friends. Well, she wasn't going to give it up. She was convinced it was working. Her parents had both been so appreciative—her mother had commented several times on how organized Maeve had been this week, and her father thanked her like crazy for helping with dinner. To be honest, Maeve thought things were already going better at home. All four of them were eating dinner together, just like they used to—but now, without any arguing. Her parents were being extra nice to each other. The whole household seemed to be running really smoothly. Nobody was even talking about D-day, as Maeve had come to think of it. Sunday. Departure Day. Dad Moves Out. Maybe they'd already changed their minds!

So then why, a little voice inside her said, *is Dad still packing boxes every afternoon?*

But she pushed that thought away. The boxes were all being stored down in the cinema. She didn't think there was anything that would give Isabel or Katani reason to think her parents were up to something.

In fact, her mom was helping Sam with his homework when the girls got back to Maeve's apartment. Her mom couldn't have been nicer, Maeve thought. She offered them all chocolate chip cookies, and when they told her what they were doing, she even said Maeve could borrow anything she wanted from her closet.

Not, Maeve thought, *that there's much in there I'd want.* But it was still awfully nice of her.

"Your mom seems different," Katani said ten minutes later, once the door to Maeve's room was closed behind them. "Calmer, I guess. Don't you think?"

"She's gone back to work part-time," Maeve said. THAT much she could tell her friends! "I think she likes it. She says she can get all of her organization mania out of her system at the office. So she's much more easygoing at home."

Isabel was cooing over Maeve's guinea pigs. "Omigosh, they are SO sweet," she said, leaning over the top of the cage. "What are their names, again? I keep forgetting."

"That's because she changes them every week!" Katani laughed.

Maeve smiled. "They're still Romeo and Juliet. And they have been for a whole six days. I haven't figured out who they're going to be next week."

Katani was already past the guinea pigs, diving into Maeve's closet. "Okay ..." she mumbled. "Do you think you want something kind of subdued and elegant, or something that screams LOOK AT ME?"

"Well, you know me. It's gotta be the 'look at me' look," Maeve told her. "And it's gotta be pink!"

Isabel giggled. "You'd never know that," she said ironically, looking around at Maeve's room, which was more pink than any place she'd ever seen.

Katani was digging furiously through a pile of tops on Maeve's chair. Maeve had to admit that her model daughter behavior hadn't exactly crept into her bedroom yet. She still thought that piling clothes on her chair made a lot more sense than hanging them in her closet. What was the point? You could never find anything that way!

"THIS," Katani said at last, pulling out a silvery-pink satin top with a great V-neck. "Oh, Maeve, this is totally great. Now all we have to do is figure out some kind of skirt, and you're all set."

For the next hour, Maeve forgot all about her family, having to be a perfect daughter, and figuring out what she wanted to know about her past. Instead, she felt like Cinderella. She didn't know how Katani did it, but somehow she pulled out one thing and then another thing ... clothes Maeve might never have considered wearing together ... and the next thing she knew, she looked like a model! Katani just made you feel good inside and out.

The complete outfit was amazing. Katani found a slim black skirt wedged in the back of Maeve's closet, and a pair of strappy black sandals. The effect with the silvery top was absolutely perfect.

"And if you'll let me, I'll do your hair," Isabel said. "I've been making hair combs as presents lately. I take those metal hair combs from the drugstore and add beads and jewels to them. I can custom-design one to go with your top." She pulled Maeve's hair over to one side. "See? You look like you belong in Hollywood."

Maeve felt inspired to leap up on her bed, pretending it was a stage. "Okay, you guys. If I win, what do you think of this as an acceptance speech?

"First," she said, clearing her throat, "I want to thank all of my friends who made tonight possible. Katani Summers, Goddess of the Sewing Machine and Designer Extraordinaire. If it weren't for Katani, the blankets would have come out looking like starfish."

"That's so true," Isabel cried.

Maeve held up one hand. "Wait! I'm not done. And thanks to Isabel Martinez, who dove right into this project even though she was brand new to our school. And gave it her all. And loaned her artistic vision and made the blankets absolutely beautiful!"

Isabel and Katani clapped as Maeve went on to thank Charlotte and Avery—even though they weren't there to hear their virtues celebrated.

"You're a natural, Maeve," Isabel said warmly. "I can just see you up there on stage now. I bet you're going to win," she added.

Maeve blinked. The imaginary stage vanished, and she was back in her own bedroom, facing her smiling friends. Reality came flooding back.

Well, she sure hoped that she won. She HAD to win. She was counting on it ... and not because she wanted a chance to be in the spotlight, either. It just seemed more important now, more important than anything.

ଔ

Isabel had her materials laid out on the kitchen table. Hair combs, beads of all different sizes, and top-quality glue. She wanted to make Maeve an absolutely beautiful comb to wear in her hair on Friday. Isabel adored this kind of project. She loved choosing just the right mixture of stones and silver, to complement the top Maeve would be wearing. Yes, amethyst, it would be—amethyst, which would look amazing with her hair.

She was concentrating so hard that she almost didn't hear her mother come in. Late afternoons lately had been the hardest time for her mother, who was still getting used to the medicine they were giving her to keep her from getting another flare-up from multiple sclerosis.

"That looks lovely," her mother said, pulling up a chair. "Are you making that for anyone special?"

Isabel told her mother all about Maeve. "She really deserves this award, Mama. She worked so hard on those blankets, and she got so many others to help her with the project." Isabel smiled, slipping a purple gem into place. "She's so ... oh, I don't know the best way to describe her!" She shook her head. "She has such an amazing spirit. She really always includes other people ... she's got such a big heart!"

Her mother smiled, watching Isabel work.

"And you know something, Mama," Isabel said slowly, "I think something has really been bothering her lately and she hasn't wanted to burden anyone with it. Do you know what I mean?"

"Have you asked her?" her mother wondered. "Maybe she just needs to know that you want to hear."

Isabel shook her head. She knew that in her mother's world, this was true. But sometimes Isabel felt like her mother didn't understand HER world. Things were so different for her than they had been for her mother, who grew up in a very protected household in suburban Michigan, filled with lots of extended family. And, all of her mother's friends knew Spanish and most of them were from Mexico, too. This wasn't true for Isabel. Her friends were from all over. They were all so different ... from each other, and from Isabel.

"Well, you can let her know that you're there for her," her mother said slowly. She almost seemed to be reading Isabel's mind. "That much is true around the world."

Isabel put the comb carefully aside. She looked at her mother's lovely face, which was still so beautiful even though she looked tired from the medicine. "Mama, what was it like for you when you were my age?" she asked. She was thinking about her project for Ms. O'Reilly. This was such a rare chance, to have her mother up and eager to talk. She wanted to take advantage of it.

Her mother smiled. "Well, you know that I was one of six children. Not like you and Elena Maria. We were a big family and we had to share everything. And we lived in a small house. So it was always all of us, all together. And my cousins lived two doors away. We ate dinner together almost every night, either at their place or ours. Lourdes and I, we were the babies. We had to run to catch up with our older brothers!" Her mother laughed. "We had so many brothers and cousins, we didn't really need friends the way that you girls do today." She shrugged. "It was different. Our worlds revolved around family, church, and school—in that order. When your grandfather started earning enough, Lourdes and I went to a convent school about three miles from our house. We wore uniforms ... gray-and-blue-checked skirts, and navy tops. Every day."

"And what about Papa? How did you meet Papa?" Isabel loved hearing this story, even though she knew it by heart.

"At a dance." Her mother's eyes shone. Even after all these years, Isabel's parents still adored each other. "He wanted to ask my friend to dance first. Nina. I could've killed her! But she was dancing with someone else, and he asked me ... and the rest," her mother said with a smile, "you know too well."

Isabel looked down at the comb she was working on. She wondered what material object she could bring to school to represent her family and its history. It was such a weird thing that her mother had this illness now that made her muscles weak. Because the one word that Isabel would choose to describe her mother was "strong." Her mother was quiet but had so much wisdom about life. *Like glue*, Isabel thought with a smile, turning the comb that she'd made over in her hands. Her mother was like the glue in her comb—she held them all together.

Maybe she was right about Maeve, Isabel thought. Maybe Maeve DID need to know that her friends were there for her. And whatever was on her mind—and Isabel knew that something was—they would be there. They were the Beacon Street Girls and Isabel was so happy to be one of them. They all stuck together ... like glue!

CHAPTER

11

In the Spotlight

BREAKING THE NEWS

It was Maeve's idea to get ready in the Tower on Friday night.

She told Charlotte that she thought it would be good luck. The truth was, she didn't want to risk her friends finding out about her parents splitting up. Not tonight. And her father's boxes were actually spilling out of the cinema now—there were already a few stacked up in the hallway.

So to the Tower it was. Katani had brought her sewing machine over in case they needed any last-minute alterations. By six o'clock, the room looked like a tornado had hit. Clothes were everywhere. Makeup bags, bottles of gel and mousse, curling irons ... and Charlotte had propped up a big mirror so that Maeve could see herself from every angle.

"Look at this place!" Avery shrieked, picking up a curling iron. "It looks like one of those fashion magazines Maeve's always reading. Yikes, this thing is smoking!" she exclaimed, dropping the iron like a hot potato.

Maeve laughed. It was true—the Tower was strewn with

clothes, her bag of hair equipment, shoes kicked off everywhere, and vials and jars and bottles all over the place.

"It looks like a movie star's dressing room," Isabel said, coming over to Maeve and putting her hand on her arm. "We're so proud of you, Maeve."

Maeve felt tears rush to her eyes. Don't, she thought. Don't say another nice thing to me or I'm going to lose it.

"To Maeve!" Avery exclaimed, grabbing one of Maeve's high heels and lifting it up like a glass. "Maeve Kaplan-Taylor, we are proud to have you as our friend."

Later, Maeve couldn't say why that one gesture completely undid her. Maybe it was because she'd been trying so hard to keep her parents' news a secret from her friends, and she felt bad about that. Maybe it was just the days and days of bottling up her feelings. In any case, her emotions just came bursting free, and before she knew it, she was sobbing. Absolutely sobbing. Isabel jumped up to put her arms around her, and then Katani and Charlotte were hurrying over to hug her, and Avery was staring with bewilderment and concern at the shoe in her hand.

"What?" Avery managed. "Did I say something I shouldn't have? Is there something wrong with this shoe? What did I DO?"

Maeve wiped her tear-stained face, shaking her head, half-laughing and half-crying. "You're so silly," she told Avery. "It isn't YOU. It's—well, my parents told me and Sam that they're separating."

"Separating?" Katani repeated dumbly, staring at Maeve as if she couldn't believe her ears. "Are you sure?"

Everyone looked stunned.

"Yes," Maeve said sadly. "I'm SURE. I wish I weren't."

Nobody seemed to know what to say for a moment.

Then Avery, still holding Maeve's shoe, made her pronouncement.

"That stinks," she said, with her well-meaning directness. "Has your dad already moved out?"

Maeve shook her head. "Not yet. It's supposed to happen this weekend," she said, grabbing for a box of tissues and starting to cry all over again.

Isabel engulfed Maeve in a huge hug. "So that's why you've been acting different. I kind of thought something was wrong," she said.

"You did?" Maeve blinked. "Really?"

Katani was pacing back and forth. "Maeve, WHY DIDN'T YOU TELL US?"

"Maybe she wasn't ready to talk about it yet," Isabel said defensively. She hated the thought of anyone being mad at Maeve right now. Katani gave Isabel a look. She wanted to hear whatever Maeve was thinking from Maeve, and not from Isabel.

"I'm sorry," Maeve sniffled. "To tell you the truth, I've kind of been hoping that they'd change their minds."

"They hardly ever do that," Avery said bluntly.

"... I don't know. I feel like maybe part of this was my fault," Maeve said brokenly. "You know how flaky I can be about assignments and grades and stuff. They were always getting in arguments about me. I figured if I were on my best behavior, if I tried harder to help out, if I just did better in school ..."

"Ah HA!" Katani cried. "So that's why you've been super-organized lately!"

Avery set Maeve's shoe down. "Maeve, I hate to burst your bubble," she said matter-of-factly, "but it isn't all about you. Parents don't split up because of kids. Trust me on this.

They do it because they are unhappy themselves. It took me a long time to realize it. The good news is it's not your fault they want to split up. The bad news is that there is not a whole lot you can do to change it."

Maeve blotted at her face with a tissue. "I don't know," she said, her voice wobbly. "I think they actually are changing their minds, Avery. Really."

"Well, it'll probably be the first time in history if that happens," Avery told her. "Really, Maeve. I hope they do, but just don't count on it, okay? Take care of yourself. It's what your parents want you to do. It'll take a while, but you'll be okay," she added. "When my mom and dad split up, it was awful. But kids can get through it when they have friends and their parents love them. Kids are resilient. I know. Look at me."

Resilient, Maeve thought. There was that word again. That's what her father had said, too.

But right now, Maeve didn't want to be resilient. She wanted her parents to stay together.

"People get back together in the movies," Maeve said stubbornly. "Haven't you ever seen *The Parent Trap*? Or *What a Girl Wants*? Or *Three Smart Girls*?"

"Those are MOVIES, Maeve," Avery retorted. "Not real life."

Charlotte looked at her watch. "Hey, we have to get Maeve to the Community Center."

"Oh, no!" Maeve gasped, rushing over to peer into the mirror. "I look AWFUL. I can't go looking like this!"

"Katani, do you have your magic makeup bag with you?" Charlotte asked.

Katani nodded. "Charlotte, run down and get some ice. We have to bring the swelling down around her eyes," she said briskly, opening up her makeup bag and taking out a few bottles and tubes. When Katani worked her makeup magic, she sounded more like a scientist than a makeup artist.

It helped Maeve to have something to focus on. Right now, there didn't seem to be that much more to say about what she was going through. The girls just wanted to help her get to the awards ceremony feeling better and looking more or less like her regular self.

Isabel noticed that Maeve's fingers were trembling as she tried to smooth back her hair.

"Hey," she said softly, taking out the comb she'd made for her. "Maybe this is a good time to give you this."

And with a few deft strokes, Isabel had helped pull Maeve's hair back from her face and slipped the comb in. It was beautiful. The purple and silver beads looked lovely with Maeve's silvery top, and they helped bring out the blue in her eyes. Best of all, the comb actually got a smile out of Maeve.

"You MADE this?" she said, gazing wonderingly at the comb in the mirror. "Isabel, you are so talented, thank you!"

It was good to see her brighten up. Good to see the sparkle back in her eyes.

And that, Isabel thought as she adjusted the comb, *was what friends were for, too.* Helping to hold things together just when it seemed like everything was coming apart.

THE BIG NIGHT

Finally, Maeve was ready.

She practiced her "graceful acceptance walk" going down the stairs from the Tower, noticing that her new platform heels made her a lot taller—and a lot more wobbly. She had to hang on to the banister all the way down. Well, maybe her mom and dad would walk her up to the stage to accept her award!

IF she won, that is. Maeve could see it now, they'd be beaming at each other, each holding one of her arms. And after the awards ceremony, they'd probably want to go out alone together, just the two of them, to talk about how marvelous the whole night had been. Who could say? Maybe by tomorrow night they'd be reconsidering the whole separation idea.

She could imagine the scene in her head.

"Maeve ... Sam," her mother would say. "Your dad and I have talked it all over, and we realized we almost made the biggest mistake of our lives! Thanks to you, Maeve, we've realized that all of our problems were really trivial. We're definitely going to stay together."

"Maeve, what's the matter?" Avery demanded. "Did you twist your ankle? Why are you walking like that?"

Maeve blushed. Apparently her "graceful acceptance walk" wasn't quite as graceful as she thought.

She tried to ignore Avery. Head held high, Maeve went over one last version of her acceptance speech in her head.

Of course, the real thanks goes to the community at Jeri's Place. What an exceptional and dedicated staff! The people who work there do so much to bring warmth and comfort to the lives of the people that they serve. The blanket project only adds to their terrific service.

She could hear the deafening applause around her. In her mind's eye, she was reaching for the trophy, even bigger now than she'd imagined it earlier—her parents with their arms around each other, their eyes shining ...

"Maeve, COME ON," Avery said, grabbing her by the arm. "If we don't leave now, we're going to miss the whole thing! What if you actually win this thing? You don't want to be late to your own awards ceremony."

CR

The Junior Community Service Awards Ceremony was taking place in the Brookline Community Center. The last time the girls had been here, the room had been cleared for social dancing lessons. Today, there were dozens of rows of folding chairs set up facing a podium. A local television station was setting up cameras, and the Rotary Club, which was sponsoring the awards ceremony, was up at a small table next to several teachers from local junior high schools. Mrs. Fields, the principal of Abigail Adams and Katani's grandmother, was up at the table next to Ms. Rodriguez.

The first two rows had been cordoned off for people who were receiving awards.

"Look! They've saved seats for us," Avery exclaimed as she steered Maeve up toward the front. Isabel, Charlotte, and Katani were just behind them. Maeve couldn't believe how many people there were. She saw dozens of kids she knew from school—people had really turned out! Dillon was sitting in the fourth row, with Pete Wexler and Nick Montoya.

Maeve suddenly felt funny. She didn't know why. There were so many people here. This was her kind of night. Why did she feel shaky all of a sudden? All her life Maeve had dreamed of accepting an award ...

Maeve gulped. She twisted around in her chair, trying to find her mom and dad. Finally she saw her father, sitting with Sam several rows back. It had never actually occurred to Maeve that her mom and dad might not sit with each other. EVERYTHING was different than she'd imagined. Suddenly, Maeve felt distinctly nervous. Distinctly afraid of getting up in front of ANYONE, let alone her friends, classmates, and most of all, her parents. How were her mom and dad supposed to hug each other and reunite if they weren't even sitting in the same ROW? Everything was wrong!

But there wasn't time to agonize about this. Mrs. Fields was getting up to introduce the awards ceremony. She was welcoming all of the parents, talking about the value of community service for young people, and saying how proud they should be of all ten of the students who had been nominated for awards this evening.

She beamed out at the audience and then directly at Maeve.

"What a pleasure it is to have this opportunity tonight to acknowledge all of you who have gone out of your way to help others," Mrs. Fields said. "The students have shown so much initiative, so much optimism, and such persistence in making their dreams work for others. Thanks to their vision and leadership, we now have new programs thriving in our community. I would like to ask all of you to give them a big round of applause, and to let them know how grateful we are for the leadership they have shown.

"This is truly an instance," Mrs. Fields continued, taking off her reading glasses for a moment, "of every single one of us being a winner, thanks to the hard efforts of these distinguished young people." She beamed. "I hope you'll forgive me if I quote my favorite children's book of all time— *Miss Rumphius*—when I say that each of these students has truly made the world a more beautiful place, thanks to their creativity and hard work."

Everyone was clapping loudly. Maeve knew she should be feeling wonderful, hearing her principal saying these amazing things, but she was too busy trying to figure out where her mother was sitting. Oh—there she was. Sitting right on the other side of Sam. She settled back into her chair, nervously fiddling with her bracelet. Well, at least her mother and father were NEAR each other, even if they weren't sitting side by side.

For about fifteen minutes, one of the men from the Rotary Club read from a piece of paper about the ten kids who had been nominated. Each kid who Maeve heard about sounded more amazing than the one before. One had started a tutoring program. Another was helping to organize volunteers at a hospital. By the third description that she heard, Maeve felt pretty certain that she wasn't going to win, and she felt free to let her attention drift a little. She kept sneaking looks at her parents out of the corner of her eye.

"Our real purpose tonight is to commend all ten of these individuals," the man from the Rotary Club said. "But we wanted to give a special certificate of achievement to three of the nominees whose work, in our minds, showed unusual diligence and determination, and who truly exemplify the ideals of young adult community service."

Maeve's mouth felt dry. She really had NO idea that she'd find this whole experience so nerve-wracking.

The first award went to a boy from a junior high in Boston. His name was Simon, and he had started an after-school program teaching English to kids who spoke other languages. Everyone clapped loudly when Simon came up to accept his certificate. Maeve couldn't believe how poised and self-assured he was. He thanked a bunch of people when he made his speech, but he made it sound like he hadn't practiced at all—like he was used to getting awards every day of the week!

The second certificate went to a girl named Hannah something-or-other who had been volunteering as a coach, teaching soccer to first and second graders with special physical needs. Everyone clapped really hard for her. Because Avery knew her from soccer, she started whistling and stamping when Hannah's name was called.

Hannah came bounding up to claim her certificate, a big grin on her face. She was every bit as poised and articulate as Simon when she thanked the man from the Rotary Club who gave her the award. Maeve had to hand it to her. Like Simon, she looked completely natural and at ease. She said a bunch of things about the kids she coached and how inspiring they were, and people kept clapping and clapping.

Maeve could feel her hands growing sweaty ... just like Riley Lee's had been when they'd danced together a few weeks ago. Being on stage never bothered Maeve before. This was so strange. All of a sudden she just wanted to go home.

"Thank you, Hannah," Mrs. Fields said, getting to her feet with a smile. "And finally, our third certificate of merit goes to ..." There was an expectant pause. "Maeve Kaplan-Taylor, for her Project Thread. Maeve encouraged a group of students to make blankets for children living in a homeless shelter. These special gifts touched their hearts and made a tangible difference to their lives."

Maeve couldn't believe her ears. She sat completely frozen, as if she were glued to her chair.

"Maeve—you WON!" Avery shrieked, practically in her ear. "You've got to go up there and get your certificate! GO!"

Maeve felt like she couldn't move. Her feet seemed to be made of lead. What had happened to the graceful acceptance walk that she'd practiced? It took both Avery and Katani tugging at her arms to pull her out of her seat. She felt like every word in the English language went right out of her head as she stumbled up to the podium. Mrs. Fields was beaming down at her, looking proud and happy.

She handed Maeve a large certificate, gesturing for her to come over to the podium to say something.

Maeve blinked. Here it was—her chance to make her speech. She tried desperately to remember what she wanted to say. Come on, she scolded herself. You rehearsed this! She knew that she wanted to thank people. Her parents. Her friends. The kids at Jeri's Place. Thank you to ... to ...

"Um," Maeve said into the microphone. It made a scratching sound, and she jumped back. The faces in the auditorium swam in front of her. "Um—thank you. Thanks," she said. And that was it. That was all she said! Not to mention the fact that she almost tripped on her way back down from the stage. Those platform shoes, Maeve thought; they get you every time.

Her face was flaming red. She could feel it.

"Way to go, Maeve," Avery whispered, patting her arm. "You're awesome."

"Good job," Charlotte said with a big smile.

Isabel's eyes were shining.

And Katani—who NEVER hugged in public—actually broke out of character and engulfed her in a warm hug.

Her friends kept patting her warmly on the shoulder as she took her seat again. Her palms felt damp and her heart was pounding. Wow—who knew that this could happen? Maeve had always assumed that stage fright was just something that happened in books. Maybe it was the stress about her parents ... she wasn't sure. For once in her life, Maeve understood the phrase "tongue-tied." That was exactly what it had felt like up there—as if her tongue were tied in knots.

"Good job up there. Nice and short," Avery said comfortingly.

"I choked up," Maeve whispered. "I totally blew it."

"But you won," Katani reminded her. "Way to go, Maeve."

Her friends all wanted to inspect her certificate. Everyone passed it around, admiring it, but Maeve was feeling worse by the minute. "I meant to thank you guys," she whispered. "I meant to thank LOTS of people, and I didn't. I feel terrible."

"Maeve, don't worry," Isabel said, giving Maeve a quick hug. "We're just proud of you, okay?"

The awards ceremony was coming to a close, and before Maeve knew it, her classmates were swarming around her. Betsy and Abby and Riley and Nick ... it was hard for anyone to get close, so many kids were trying to come up and say congratulations! She saw Dillon, hanging back with Pete and Nick, and her cheeks reddened again. WHY couldn't she have said something suave and eloquent up there? She'd had her big moment, and she'd CHOKED!

"Nice job, Maeve," Dillon said. To Maeve's amazement, he looked slightly embarrassed. Dillon Johnson—blushing? Now there was a first. "Seriously," he said, raising his eyes and meeting hers. "That's really cool, Maeve."

Even through the haze of her embarrassment, Maeve couldn't help registering the fact that Dillon had actually COME UP TO HER and said something nice. This was a big milestone.

"Thanks," Maeve said, making major eye contact and playing up the moment for all it was worth. Okay, she'd blown it up on the podium; that didn't mean she couldn't try to make up for it now.

"Maybe," Dillon said, leaning closer and lowering his voice, "We could go out and celebrate sometime."

Maeve's heartbeat quickened. "Uh ... that would be nice.

I'd like that," she said, without missing a beat. Well thank heavens her ability to speak had come back to her NOW. Dillon Johnson had asked her out! Right there in the Community Center! Maeve thought she might quite possibly die of joy right on the spot. Dillon was already being pulled away by Pete and Nick, but Maeve kept her eyes on his back as they left the room. Maybe the night wasn't a complete disaster after all. Her stomach was a little more settled now.

"Maeve!" It was her mom, coming up to her with a huge smile on her face. "Oh, honey—congratulations! I'm so proud of you!"

Her parents! In all her excitement and embarrassment, Maeve had almost forgotten her secret mission tonight. "Where's Daddy?" she said, as her mother gave her a quick hug.

She needn't have asked—he was right behind her, looking as proud and happy as she could imagine. As proud and happy as her mom.

"I always knew that blanket project was a great idea," her father said with a huge smile on his face.

Maeve hugged him, but she could see her mother's expression change. Uh-oh—this wasn't such a good remark on her father's part. Her mother had been critical of the blanket project, thinking that it was taking way too much of Maeve's time. She'd better change the subject before—

But it was too late.

"You know, Ross, I ALSO liked Maeve's blanket project. Please don't say that in that kind of voice," her mother retorted in a low, hurt voice.

"Carol, this isn't about you! I was actually talking to Maeve!" her father said, irritated.

Maeve winced. She didn't want them arguing. Not here!
This was definitely not the way that things were
supposed to happen.

"You guys," she said quickly, putting her hand on each
parent's arm. "Can we go out for ice cream somewhere to
celebrate? Just the four of us?"

Her parents exchanged glances. "Sure," her mother said
at last. But she didn't sound ecstatic about it.

Her father was quiet on the way to the car, too. But
Maeve ignored that.

Tonight may not have been perfect, but it was pretty
darned close. She'd actually won the award! Every time she
looked at the certificate she felt a thrill go through her. She'd
done a good job—a terrific job in fact! And everyone that she
cared about was there to celebrate her success. And to top it
off, Dillon had asked her out.

Okay, maybe her parents were a little touchy around each
other. But Maeve assured herself that they were just worn
out from the tensions of the week. She couldn't believe that
her father would still go along with his plan to move out on
Sunday. Not now. Not when she'd been the perfect model
daughter—and even one with an award to prove it!

∞

Montoya's was packed with kids after the awards
ceremony, so Maeve suggested that they go to an old favorite
of hers—the Ice Cream Shoppe, a wonderful, '50s-style diner
that served ice cream sundaes at an old-fashioned counter.
She noticed that her mother sat at the fourth stool and her
father at the first, leaving her and Sam to sit in between them.
And after the first delicious bites of ice cream, Maeve started
to sense that maybe this hadn't been the best plan. Her

mother was subdued, and her father kept directing most of his conversation to Maeve or Sam.

Finally, her mother cleared her throat. "I know this is a celebration tonight, Maeve. But we should probably talk a little bit about what's happening this weekend. Would you two like to help Dad move some things over to the new place tomorrow?"

Her father looked searchingly at Maeve and Sam. "I'd really appreciate your help," he said. "And if you come over tomorrow and help me move, you'll already know the place a little bit by Sunday. I was hoping you'd have dinner with me there on Sunday night."

Maeve's ears buzzed. This was real. It was really going to happen.

"Maeve?" Her father put his hand over hers. "Are you okay?"

Maeve felt foolish. Had she really thought that she could get them to change their minds? Just by being helpful? Just by winning an award?

Avery was right. Parents did what they were going to do no matter what. She'd been unbelievably naive to think otherwise.

"I'll help move boxes!" her brother said, polishing off his ice cream. Sam looked perfectly fine with the idea. Or at least USED to the idea by now.

That's because he's admitted it to himself, Maeve thought. He hasn't been dreaming all week, the way I have, that they'll change their minds. Her brother was little, but he was a realist. Maeve blinked back tears. She was such a dreamer. She always thought she could change the world.

Well, this time it looked like she couldn't. No matter what she did, her parents were going to go ahead with this.

And Maeve didn't see what she could possibly do to make things better.

CR

"What's the matter?" her father asked late that night, when Maeve padded down to the kitchen in her favorite slippers. "You can't sleep either?"

Maeve shook her head, pulling a chair up to the kitchen table.

"How about some warm milk with cinnamon and honey?"

She nodded. It was her father's specialty—and it almost always soothed her enough to help her get sleepy again. She couldn't remember the last time that he'd made it for her; she realized that this might never happen again. Not the same way. Coming downstairs and finding her dad here. All four of them together in one house.

"Hey, kiddo," he said, putting his hand under her chin and lifting her face up so that his eyes met hers. "You doing okay?"

Maeve's eyes swam with tears. "It's just that I thought you and Mom would change your minds when you saw how smoothly things were going and how much better I was doing with everything. I didn't think you'd really go through with this."

Her father nodded. That was one of the things that Maeve adored about her father—she could really tell him whatever was on her mind, and he didn't get freaked out. He liked to say that he was hard to shock, and it was true.

"That's kind of understandable. I think Mom and I feel a little bit the same way. We didn't really think it would come to this either. Maeve, this is hard. We can't pretend it isn't."

"Why can't you just stay?" Maeve asked, the tears

❁ 113 ❁

spilling over her cheeks. "Can't you two figure this out somehow? I know someone whose mom and dad saw a marriage counselor," she added, brushing away the tears. "And they said it helped!"

"We've been seeing a counselor," her father told her. "And we're going to keep seeing her, Maeve. But she also thinks that this is a good idea. We're at the point where we just need to stand back and see ourselves and each other for who we really are. We're hoping that living apart for a while will let us do that better."

Her father went over to the stove to start heating up some milk. Maeve wanted to keep this moment frozen in time forever. But she knew she couldn't. "Dad," she said, barely trusting her voice. "Is there anything that Sam and I can do to help? You know ... to help you and Mom figure it out?"

Her father sighed. "I'm afraid this one is up to us, Maeve. But you CAN do something. Something really important: Don't blame yourself. Don't burden yourself by thinking that it's up to you to make us get along better. Try to be honest about your feelings. It's tough enough to go through something like this and hide how you really feel."

Maeve swallowed. She had been thinking that somehow she'd been responsible.

"And Maeve," her father added, "don't shut your friends out. You're going to need them. Now more than ever. They're there to help you, especially in hard times."

It was like he could read her mind, Maeve thought. Would that still be true after this weekend? Would they still be close, even when her father wasn't living with them anymore?

be happy  be lucky

Nests are so happy comfy!

Part Two
Putting It Back Together

CHAPTER
12

Moving Day

❧ . . . .

Notes to Self:
1. Remember: DO NOT freak out if Dad's
   new place is v. small. Don't make
   him feel any worse about this than he
   already does.
2. HOW small is small??? I know he said
   two bedrooms. I know I'm going to have
   to share a room with my brother. BUT—
   HOW SMALL IS SMALL???
3. Remember: Bring movie star posters for
   my half of the bedroom wall. Avery
   says it's important to make your
   bedroom in your other house feel like
   home. Also bring pink beanbag chair.
   Can use as a divider between me and
   Sam. Also bring old boom box. Can be
   repaired. Also teen mags. Need them.

4. Remember: a pack of cards. Don't know
   why this is a good idea but Avery says
   it's WAY IMPORTANT for the first day.
   And she should know. She's been there.
5. Was Dillon serious about going out?
   Find this out somehow. Be v. subtle.
   Get Katani to ask him.

Phew. Maeve took a deep breath. She looked around her bedroom one last time to see if there was anything else she could take over with her to her new room at Dad's apartment. She and Sam weren't staying over tonight—they were just going to have dinner with Dad, and then come back home. Next weekend would be their first time sleeping over at his new place. But Maeve was still nervous. She hadn't seen her dad's place yet. Last weekend Maeve's mother had taken Sam and Maeve downtown for lunch and a trip to Filene's Basement while her dad rented a U-Haul to move over a few big pieces of furniture. Maeve was glad she did. It would have been too sad to see furniture leaving the house. Today they would just head over in the car, with a few odds and ends. Her dad's philodendrons—how was it possible to keep a couple of plants alive since college?—and his collection of LPs, or "vinyls," as he liked to call them. Her dad was a pack rat, like Maeve. He hated throwing anything out.

"Okay, you two. Let's go check this place out," her father said, coming upstairs to get Maeve and Sam. The Taurus was packed up, and they were ready to go.

Maeve threw a parting kiss to her guinea pigs. This morning she had renamed them Ben and Jen. "I loved *Alias*," she explained on I.M. to Katani and Isabel.

"Don't worry, babies. I'm only going to be a few hours,"

she cooed. She scooped each one up for one last snuggle and tickled Jen's tummy.

Guinea pigs, she thought affectionately, are fabulous. Truly a girl's best friend.

"Maeve, come on," Sam whined. "They can't understand you. They're RODENTS."

Maeve glared at him, sweeping down the stairs and hurrying outside to the sidewalk, where her father was waiting. What did her brother know? Maeve's guinea pigs were very sensitive creatures, she was sure of it. When she was sad, they drooped. When she was happy, they scampered all over their cage! Today, Dad's moving day, was unquestionably a "Drooping Day."

So this was it. Her dad was moving out.

The strangest thing was how low-key it felt. Her mom had disappeared on an "errand"—now THAT was clearly planned, Maeve thought. And her dad was acting like they were just driving down the street. Which they were, in a sense, but still ...

How do you mark things like this? Maeve thought. How do you manage to make something this important feel big enough, without falling apart?

It was hard getting into the car. Sam started to cry, and her father couldn't look at either of them. Maeve took a deep breath.

The trick really was pretending that everything was okay. Maybe you got through tough moments like this by forcing yourself to believe that somehow they really WEREN'T that tough.

It was like acting—that's all. All she had to do was swallow hard and pretend like she was going on a cool trip.

"Come on," she said, trying for what sounded like an

upbeat tone. "Dad isn't moving to Mars, Sam. Okay? It's just Washington Square—less than a mile away. And we're going to be over all the time! So much you're going to be sick of us, Dad!" she assured her father, giving his arm a warm squeeze.

Her dad looked as choked up as Sam.

Great. Looked like she was going to have to be the strong one here.

Maeve picked up the duffel bag her father had left on the sidewalk, peering into the back of the car to see if there was any space left. But the bag weighed a ton, and she quickly set it down.

"What do you have in here, Dad? It feels like rocks," Maeve said, staggering backward under the weight of the bag.

"Um—photographs. Scrapbooks and stuff," her dad said. "Mostly photographs of you and Sam."

"Oh, Daddy," Maeve said. Her voice wobbled and all her acting powers seemed to be getting her nowhere. It almost broke her heart, thinking of her dad going through the photographs ... picking out ones to take with him. But when she saw Sam start to sniffle again, she drew herself up as tall as she could and tried again. Once they were in the car, it would be easier, she told herself. Once they were really on their way.

Her father's new apartment was in a brick building with gables on Washington Street. The building was what her father called a mock-Tudor—it looked old-fashioned and a little bit mysterious. Dad's apartment was on the second floor, which Maeve liked. It reminded her of their place over the Movie House.

She was amazed when her father opened up the door. It looked so moved-in! Her father had set up the living room already—three of his houseplants were even there. It was definitely not huge, but the room had a pretty fireplace and nice high ceilings. At the end of the living room was a kind of nook with a small kitchen in it. Her father said it was called a "galley kitchen," after the kinds of kitchens used on ships. There wasn't a lot of room, but her dad had set it all up so neatly—pots, pans, glasses, plates—that Maeve thought it looked almost cozy.

"Not bad, Dad," Sam said admiringly.

Maeve was pretty impressed, too. Her father had even set the table in the kitchen. He'd knocked himself out, getting things ready for them. She felt a lump forming in her throat, but she fought back tears. It was just ... well, it was so touching to see what he'd done to make them feel comfortable here. He'd even brought over some of Sam's video games, and Maeve saw the latest issue of *People* magazine on the coffee table.

"Daddy, this is nice," Maeve said.

It helped having seen the living room first. Next came her father's bedroom. It was small, but had a nice view of the garden below. Maeve noticed that there were pictures of her and Sammy everywhere. It looked like her dad had put those out first thing!

"And now—" her father said, throwing open the door to the room across the hallway. "TA-DAH!" Maeve had to laugh. He sounded just like her. The whole performance thing was definitely "in the genes," as her mother would say. That and making things happy and nice for other people.

She turned to look in the room ... then gulped. This was going to take some courage. The room was cute, but no kidding—it was SMALL. Avery's Closet Number One was probably bigger than this. Her dad had set up bunk beds on one wall, which made Sam go into whoops of ecstasy. Not that there was much choice, there wasn't room to fit two beds in side by side. Maeve had to summon up every single ounce of acting skill she had. Think of Sara Crewe in *The Little Princess*, she told herself. Think of Audrey Hepburn in *Sabrina*, before she goes to Paris. Think of Drew Barrymore in *Ever After*. Think of every noble, suffering, I-have-to-live-in-a-garret-but-I'm-still-a-princess movie that you can.

Of course, most garrets only come with rats ... not with an eight-year-old brother.

"Daddy, this ROCKS!" Sam yelled, hurling himself up the ladder and onto the top bunk.

Maeve took a deep breath. "Sam," she said, as calmly as she could, "you and I are going to talk LATER about how we're going to divide the room." She dragged in her pink beanbag chair, which filled one entire corner. "The pink side is going to be MINE."

Her father shook his head with a rueful smile. "I know it's a small room. Will you two be okay in here?"

Something about the tone in his voice made Maeve forget all about how small the room was and how on EARTH she was going to deal with sharing a bedroom with the Military Maniac. Her dad looked so woebegone and so worried all of a sudden that all she cared about was making him feel better.

Maeve flung her arms around her father, forgetting all about the bunk beds and her brother and the unbearable question of which was worse, having Sam on the top bunk snoring over her head or on the bottom bunk where he could kick her mattress and send her flying. "Dad, it's fine. It's sweet," Maeve assured him.

"I think it's the coolest," Sam announced. "I'm gonna put my posters ALL OVER. And I'm—"

"Sam," Maeve said calmly, hoping to defer this conversation until later, "I think we better go help Dad with dinner."

This was NOT the time to squash her younger brother. Not on their first night here. And thank heavens, they didn't have to spend the night here. Not yet. Maeve would have all week to Sam-proof herself before she had to endure THAT.

Dinner was actually nice. Her father had made their all-time favorite—American Chop Suey. It was macaroni, ground beef, tomato sauce ... and totally delicious. It felt funny sitting at the small table in the kitchen and eating there, just the three of them, but not funny as in BAD—just new. They talked about a bunch of stuff. Maeve's award ceremony. Things coming up at school. The baseball play-offs. Dinner seemed to fly by, but as soon as they were finished eating, an awkward silence descended.

Maeve wondered if Sam was thinking the same thing she was. What now?

Dad's TV wasn't set up yet. Neither was his stereo. The living room was feeling quieter and quieter. Maeve's eye flew to the new issue of *People* magazine on the coffee table. If she were at home, she'd be running off to her room to I.M. her friends or to read that enticing magazine. But here at Dad's she felt more like she was VISITING. You couldn't just go off and read a magazine when you were (sort of) a guest, could you?

But what else were the three of them supposed to do?

All of a sudden, Maeve remembered Avery's tip.

"Anyone want to play cards?" she asked, taking the cards out of the pocket of her jacket. Thank you, Avery Madden, she thought. YOU WERE SO RIGHT.

"Poker!" Sam shrieked, looking like he'd just won the lottery.

Maeve wanted to play Spit, so they flipped for it, and she won. Before she knew it, the three of them were sitting on the living room floor, hands flying, laughing their heads off. Maeve even forgot about acting brave. The truth was, she was having a good time. Okay, the bedroom situation was a little less than perfect. But she liked her dad's new place. It obviously had good karma—Maeve won every single game.

JOINT CUSTODY

"So how was it?" Avery asked, in her usual blunt manner. "What's your dad's new place like?"

It was Monday at lunch, and the girls were catching up on the weekend.

Mostly, though, they wanted to know how Maeve was doing. How the move had gone, and how she was feeling about it all.

"I can't lie—my bedroom over there is the size of your closet, Avery. AND I have to share it with Junior Military Man," Maeve said, dipping a carrot stick into some hummus. "But Dad's made it look nice. And once I figure out what goes where, it may be okay." She shrugged. "It's just weird, that's all. With my mom working part-time and my dad not there ... well, there's all this STUFF to do."

"What do you mean?" Isabel asked.

Maeve's cheeks turned pink. "I know this is going to sound awful," she confessed, "but I'm not used to doing stuff like laundry and helping with dinner. Mom's always done all of that."

Isabel nodded sympathetically. "Since my mom's been taking this medicine, she has ZERO energy. And Elena Maria claims she has too much homework. So guess who ends up doing all the dishes? ME!"

Maeve was surprised to discover that her friends all shared her pain when it came to household chores. Charlotte and her dad took turns cooking dinner. Katani said she had to help with laundry. "With four girls, you wouldn't believe how much there is to do," she told Maeve. "Of course Patrice has to wash something if it so much as TOUCHES her body." She grimaced. "And since I'm the designated neat freak, everyone always wants me to fold their stuff. I have these tricks so you don't even need to iron."

"Well, I'm drafting Sam to help," Maeve announced. "There's no reason he can't fold laundry. Even if he IS the messiest kid on the planet." She giggled. "I'll just tell him it's like folding up war maps. Then he'll love it!"

The conversation turned serious for a moment. "Are you doing okay, Maeve?" Isabel asked, her dark eyes concerned.

Maeve nodded. "You know," she said slowly, "I've been so stressed out about Dad moving out. And now that it's happened ... I mean, it's sad and everything ... but I kind of feel like the worst is over. You know what I mean?"

"Still, it's probably good to keep busy," Charlotte said thoughtfully. "Why don't we all plan a sleepover at my house on Friday night? We haven't done that in ages!"

Everyone was excited about this. Katani said she could come, and so could Isabel and Avery. "A Tower party!" everyone cried.

"I can't," Maeve said with a sigh. "I'm supposed to go over to my dad's. But you guys go ahead," she insisted, though the other girls suggested they wait for another time. "No, really, go ahead," Maeve said, despite her friends' protests. "I'll call from my dad's. And you guys can give me moral support over the phone. Come on, you guys, I'm FINE." Avery, Katani, Charlotte, and Isabel gave each other uncertain looks.

"You may think you're more fine than you really are," Avery announced. "Some days you're okay. Other days you think you will be sad forever. But my mother says 'time heals almost everything.' And she's right. So just don't ask too much of yourself, okay?"

Maeve nodded. "I know. Poor Jen and Ben. I think they know there's tension in the house. They didn't even want to eat their lettuce this morning," she said sadly.

Avery was staring at her. "Maeve," she said suddenly, as if she'd just had the most brilliant idea in the world. "Let me take care of the guinea pigs for awhile!"

"WHAT?" Maeve asked, putting down her carrot. "Avery, wasn't it bad enough giving your mother hives from Marty last weekend? You can't bring Ben and Jen home. Your mom will kill you!"

"Let me ask her," Avery pleaded. "She might say yes. I don't think she's allergic to guinea pigs, just to dogs and cats. Please, Maeve. If I bring them over and she doesn't sneeze and stuff, maybe she'd at least let me get a guinea pig one day."

"Well," Maeve said doubtfully, "you'd have to check with her, Avery. No more hiding pets over at your place."

"I'll ask," Avery agreed. "But if she says okay, can I keep them for a little while? Please?"

Maeve thought about this. On the one hand, she'd really miss Ben and Jen. They were her soul mates, and she didn't really want to be without them, even for a little while. But this was going to be a pretty busy week. She'd promised to give her mom lots of extra help after school. She had lots of lessons, and Matt was helping her with math ... and on Friday afternoon, she and Sam were going over to Dad's for their first weekend at his place. Plus, Ben and Jen needed a fair amount of looking after—changing their bedding, making sure they had clean food and lots of water. And she had all this laundry to do, and helping her mom with dinner ...

"Okay," she said, relenting. "But you HAVE to get your mom's permission, Avery. And you have to let me show you how to take care of them! Guinea pigs are completely different than dogs. They are really sensitive."

"Marty's sensitive," said Charlotte.

Avery clapped her hands together gleefully. "It'll be like joint custody," she cried. "We can share them!"

When Maeve gave her a reproachful look, Avery thought quickly. "I mean, just for this week," she added. Clearly Avery couldn't be more thrilled. Now all she had to do was to convince her mother to let her baby-sit for a pair of guinea pigs.

CHAPTER
13

The Planets Collide

aeve! Wait up!" Dillon came over just as Maeve was trying to fit her tray into the metal rack by the garbage cans.

Not exactly a romantic place to run into him. The tray started to tip, and Maeve had to grab it to keep her lunch from sliding all over the place. Food started to slosh back and forth—yuck. No wonder, Maeve thought, that not a SINGLE romantic movie gets filmed in a junior high cafeteria.

"Here, let me help," Dillon said, taking the tray and fitting it into the slot on the rack.

Be cool, she ordered herself. But it was hard, especially since Dillon looked amazingly cute today. He was wearing a pale yellow shirt and a pair of blue jeans that were a little baggy and really faded. She LOVED the way his blonde hair fell over one eye. And those eyes ... SO Orlando.

"So," he said, falling into step beside her as they walked toward the bank of seventh-grade lockers. "That award ceremony was awesome. You looked great up there, Maeve."

Maeve felt embarrassed. She may have LOOKED okay,

but she hadn't said even one percent of what she'd wanted to.

"I blew it," she told Dillon. "I meant to thank a zillion people. My friends, for helping me ... and the kids at Jeri's Place ... and my mom and dad ..."

Dillon shrugged. "Well, I thought you were great," he said loyally. "So. Want to go out and celebrate this Friday?"

Friday. Maeve couldn't believe her ears. This was for real. He was really and truly asking her out. OUT. As in—on a date! This question was not hard to answer.

"I'd love to!" she said. Beaming from ear to ear.

"Awesome!" Dillon looked happy. Happy—about going out with ME! Maeve thought. Her heart started to pound.

"I was thinking of getting some tickets to a Celtics game. My dad could drive us," Dillon went on. He started talking about some of the players ... who was injured, who they were up against. Maeve didn't exactly follow basketball, so none of what he was saying made sense to her. But she got the main point.

"Um ... you mean like the Celtics—at the Garden?" Maeve asked. That was all the way downtown.

"Yeah," said Dillon. "Are you a Celtics fan?"

When Dillon had talked about going out, she'd assumed he meant to the movies or Montoya's or some place close by. Maeve had actually never been OUT with a boy before, unless you counted The Worst Night in History with Nick Montoya. And that hadn't involved getting a ride anywhere. It just involved all Maeve's plans to have a romantic movie night with Nick going completely awry. She had wanted to see *Gone With the Wind*. He couldn't wait to get to *Spider-Man*. What a disconnect!

She knew this was different. Different as in needing to ask permission. As in needing to ask her parents. Half of Maeve's brain was thinking rationally. Just say you need to check and you'll get back to him. Not a big deal. You can even make it sound like you *might* have other plans (as if!). But the other half was excited beyond belief and didn't think about parents or asking permission or anything but saying yes right here, on the spot.

Maeve was almost dizzy with excitement. She didn't know what to think about first. What to wear ... who to tell first ... She tried to seem nonchalant as she fumbled with her locker combination. She did a rapid review of her wardrobe. Basketball game. Might be kind of chilly. Jeans and a sweater? Hair in a cute ponytail with a little Celtics cap?

She was so excited, she could barely even hear the rest of what Dillon said. It wasn't until after he'd left that Maeve suddenly remembered. Friday night was her first night staying over at Dad's place. She had completely, utterly forgotten that she had already made that commitment. They'd made plans to have dinner together first, and maybe see a movie. The three of them—Dad, Maeve, Sam. The excitement of being asked out ... on a REAL DATE ... just wiped that out of her mind, like a giant eraser. GONE.

Maeve stared at her locker dial in disbelief. How could this have happened?

Well, she couldn't let Dillon down now. No way. He was off to get tickets for the game, and she'd said she was going to go. She couldn't exactly call after him and tell him she'd made a mistake.

She'd have to explain to her dad and Sam. And they were just going to have to understand.

It's not like I can't have fun anymore, Maeve told herself quickly. Just because Dad has to move out, that doesn't mean that my whole life has to stop in its tracks. Right? If Mom and

Dad hadn't separated I'd be FREE on Friday night. I could've said yes to the sleepover with my friends when they asked ... and now to Dillon ...

If you looked at it from a certain perspective, this wasn't Maeve's fault at all. It was her parents' fault.

Maeve had a funny feeling in the pit of her stomach, but she tried to ignore it. Dillon had asked her out. This was really her first date, 'cause going to see *Gone With the Wind* with Nick ... that didn't count. She'd asked HIM, and he'd thought they were just meeting to study. This was different! A real date, with the guy she'd had a crush on for almost EVER—well a couple of weeks, but it felt like forever.

A real date. This was different.

But weren't her parents going to think this was different, too? To the tune of: Why Didn't You Ask Us First?

Maeve set her chin stubbornly. She didn't want to ask because she was afraid they might tell her that she couldn't go. They'd say that she'd already made plans with Dad and Sam, and she had to keep those plans.

She wasn't sure how to figure everything out yet, but she knew she'd think of something.

☙

Avery's Blog

Why Guinea Pigs Make Perfect Pets
1. They are small and athletic. Like me.
2. They are very well behaved—at least I
   think they are.
3. My mother isn't allergic to them.
4. My friend has two that I can borrow.
5. They are low maintenance!!!

"Mommmmm," Avery wheedled, pulling a stool up to the kitchen table, where her mother was looking through her address book, pen in hand. "Mom, PLEASE let me have them here. It's just for a week. It'll be such a big help to Maeve."

Her mother looked distracted. She was making a guest list for a big dinner party she was hosting on Saturday night. It was the last event in the Talbot Academy fund-raiser that she'd been helping to organize over the past several weeks.

"Avery, sweetie," her mother said, sounding a million miles away, "this really isn't such a good time to talk about guinea pigs ... I've got thirty people to call tonight. And after the Marty fiasco I am not sure I trust ..."

Avery swiveled on the stool, catching herself when her mother set down her pen and gave her a look that said, "Please don't swivel on the kitchen barstool."

"Mom," Avery tried again. "I swear, these little guys are totally harmless. They're in a cage. And they won't even give you allergies. I looked it up on Google. Allergies to guinea pigs are extremely rare."

Her mother sighed. "Avery, I know how much you love animals, and I am not allergic to guinea pigs, but I really don't care for rodents."

"Please," Avery begged, her voice shaking a little to keep from crying. She wanted to prove to her mother that she could be responsible for a furry pet.

Her mother looked thoughtfully at her. "Avery," she said. "Will you PROMISE to take complete care of the guinea pigs? And promise me that they'll stay in your room the entire time that they're here? In your room AND in their cage?"

Avery flung her arms around her mother. "You are the best," she whooped. "I promise, Mom. And I promise—you won't be sorry!"

Her mother sighed, turning back to her party list. "I hope not, Avery," she said. "This is a crazy week—I'm having forty people here on Saturday night for dinner. One of the biggest benefactors of Talbot Academy is coming into town, and we're having a dinner here in his honor." She took her reading glasses off and peered at Avery, an idea occurring to her. "Avery, do you think you could do me a huge favor on Saturday? Could you ask some of your friends to join us? I'd love for Mr. Jameson to meet you, and some of your friends. He was headmaster of the school when I was there and he left to work in the corporate world. He's a bit elderly, and it would be great for him to see what girls are like today." She smiled. "I think he is still a bit on the old-fashioned side, and his idea of what twelve- and thirteen-year-old girls are like might need a bit of updating."

"Sure, Mom," Avery said, hopping off the stool. "I'll ask my friends to come. And we'll be on our best behavior," she added, before her mother could even ask. "*Updated* behavior," she added. "Updated, best behavior."

If her mother was letting her bring over Ben and Ken—or whatever their names were this week—Avery could certainly help her out by showing up at her party. And if Mr. Jameson wanted to know what girls today were like, Avery and company could certainly show him an updated version!

Avery ran over to Maeve's apartment the minute her mom said yes, ready for her training session in guinea pig care. She had told Maeve she was coming later, but she didn't want to wait to get the guinea pigs. She was too worried that someone—Maeve or her mother—might change her mind. Avery wasn't going to risk that.

Maeve opened the door. She had her day planner in one

hand and her favorite feathery pen in the other. And she looked a little distracted.

"Hey," Avery said, squeezing inside without waiting to be invited. "Are you okay?"

Maeve sighed. "I just don't get this calendar stuff. No matter how hard I try, I keep planning too many things for the same day."

"Try writing notes on your mirror. That's what I do," Avery said cheerfully.

Maeve glanced at her. She wanted to pour her heart out about Friday night and Dillon and her dad and Sam, and not having asked her parents and all of that, but it occurred to her that Avery wasn't exactly the most romantic of her best friends. She could be *so* practical. She'd probably just shrug and say, "Ask them." She wouldn't see how problematic it all was. How her mom might say yes and her dad might say no. Or vice versa. Or how one or both of them might say, "Did you say yes to Dillon before asking us?" Or how likely it was that her mother would insist that she stick to her original plans. Or her father might act all hurt. Then they'd BOTH say no, and then she'd be in major trouble. Avery would never understand the complexity of it all.

Maeve had already pretty much decided it was simply too complicated to discuss this at all.

"So guess what? My mom said yes. I get to keep Ben and Jerry for a whole week!" Avery cried.

"Ben and JEN," Maeve corrected her. "I am not going to let you have them if you can't even get their names straight," she said as Avery began bounding up the stairs.

"Okay," Avery said cheerfully. She held up two little pieces of braided lanyard. "Look—I even made them leashes, so I can take them on walks."

Maeve looked horrified. "Avery!"

"Just kidding. I knew that," Avery said. "So ... can I take them home with me now?"

Maeve stared at her. She'd assumed that she'd have a little more warning than this. Besides, it wasn't at all clear from her expression how much Avery really DID know about taking care of guinea pigs.

"Give me the playbook, coach," Avery said when they got to the room. She was looking at the list of instructions Maeve had typed up earlier. Avery couldn't keep still. She was clearly excited at the prospect of her two new roommates. Lifting up the top, Avery reached into the cage and picked up a large furry ball that was asleep in the corner. "Which one is this?" she asked.

Maeve laughed and put the top back on the cage. "This is Jen. And you can't just pick them up like they're Beanie Babies or something. You have to keep the top on their cage. They need their food, and their bedding has to be changed every day. I'm going to have to give you loads of instructions."

"MAEVE! Just tell me what to do. I'll be so super-careful. I swear," Avery pleaded.

Maeve sighed. "Well, okay. I guess it'll be all right. But remember, it's only for one week. And you have to take really good care of them. Guinea pigs actually need a lot of tender loving care."

Avery read over the sheet as Maeve began ticking off instructions on her fingers. "Guinea pigs love staying in their cages but you have to keep them clean." She showed Avery the bedding material and how to change it. "You can just shred up newspaper—they don't mind."

"Yikes! You've got some story in there about the Yankees!" Avery cried. "You're going to give these guys nightmares!"

Then Maeve instructed Avery on how much food the guinea pigs would need, and what kinds of table food she could give them.

"What about Caesar salad?" Avery's mother made a great salad, and the thought of little Ben and Zen munching on a crouton was too cute for words.

"No way!" Maeve said. "You can give them a little piece of lettuce but no dressing—that would make them sick." And then as if reading Avery's mind, Maeve added, "No croutons, either."

Maeve laughed. "But listen, you really have to know this stuff." She went on, "And you can take them out to play, but be sure to keep them in a room with the door closed. And remember, you HAVE to put the top on the cage, or they'll climb out. Okay?"

"Okay. I've got it," Avery said, sticking her fingers through the bars of the cage and tickling Ben under his chin. No wonder Maeve had trouble scheduling stuff. She took too long worrying about all these little details. "Don't worry, Maeve. I'll take great care of Ben and Zen, and you'll have them back safe and sound next week. I swear."

"BEN AND JEN," Maeve corrected, feeling a little uneasy.

Avery was grinning at her own joke.

"Okay, very funny," Maeve said. "But remember, my guinea pigs are very important to me." She leaned over the cage and blew kisses at her guinea pigs, who looked a little freaked out when Avery started to hoist up the cage.

"Come on, Ben. Let's go, Jen," said Avery.

"Be careful," Maeve screeched, watching Avery as she stumbled over a pile of magazines Maeve had piled by the door. Avery recovered, barely managing to keep hold of the guinea pigs' cage. "I'll see you little guys in a week!" Maeve felt like a mother leaving her kids with a new baby-sitter. She knew there was no one more enthusiastic about the job than Avery, but still she worried. Guinea pigs were sensitive.

CHAPTER
14

Guinea Pigs Dreams

Avery's Blog

Attn: Guinea pig lovers of America:
I am babysitting my friend's guinea pigs.
I must confess, guinea pigs rule! Love
their little faces and the majorly cute
way they hold their food pellets. Do you
think guinea pigs like to race?

How to Introduce Your Guinea Pigs to a
New Environment
1. Let them crawl around and sniff their
   new room so they don't get freaked out.
2. Make their habitat cheerful and cozy.
   If they've had too much PINK in their
   old place don't worry. They'll get
   over it.
3. Get little pieces of lettuce from the
   fridge so that they don't have to eat

those gross pellets. Ask Maeve if they
can eat baby carrots.
4. They like loud music best—something
with drums.
5. KEEP YOUR DOOR CLOSED!!

Avery was up in her bedroom sitting at her desk and writing her blog. Avery's desk was cluttered with her favorite stuff, including the latest copy of *Skateboard Magazine*, the sports page from yesterday's newspaper, baseball cards, a yo-yo, and bubble gum wrappers. On the wall by her desk, Avery's bulletin board was covered with pictures of her family and friends and ticket stubs from Red Sox, Bruins, and Boston College women's basketball games. There were pictures of Avery and her dad snowboarding in Colorado, of Avery and her brothers surfing in Hawaii, and the Beacon Street Girls having a sleepover in the Tower. The rest of the walls were plastered with an enormous world map, pictures of Mia Hamm and other soccer stars, posters of her favorite dogs, and pennants of the teams she rooted for. Avery looked around her with utmost satisfaction. Her room was the one part of her house that really felt like home to her. Avery's mother loved interior decorating, which meant that almost every inch of their large colonial house was covered with beautiful upholstery, elegant drapes, and tasteful artwork.

Years ago, before Avery was old enough to stick up for herself, Avery's mom had decorated Avery's room to the max as well. Avery still had signs of all of that—she had a big mahogany four-poster bed and a dresser to match. But long ago Avery had shoved the mirror on top of the dresser over to make way for her sports trophies.

Avery had two walk-in closets, each one intended to be filled with clothes ... closets that made both Maeve and Katani positively green with envy. Avery appreciated the space, too. Just not for clothes. Closet Number One was bursting with sports gear. Shin guards, soccer balls, rollerblades, softball gloves, cleats, old uniforms, basketball sneakers, jump ropes, a boarding helmet, lacrosse sticks, a Hula Hoop, baseball caps, climbing gear, skateboards ... STUFF. Just where she needed it.

The second closet was mostly a sanctuary for Walter, Avery's snake. Now that the guinea pigs were visiting, Walter would have to stay in his tank. She liked to use this closet as a reading nook, too—she kept her old copies of comics in there, and some of her overflow trophies. And the inside wall was covered with news clippings. Avery loved the newspaper. She collected all kinds of stories, but her secret obsession was politics. Stickers from the last presidential election covered part of one wall, and a banner that said ROCK THE VOTE! Avery couldn't wait until she was old enough to vote. Only five years and ten months to go. Then she'd really make her voice matter.

Every now and then, Avery's mother would stick her head inside her room and look around with an expression of amused bewilderment. The big NO HUNTING sign that Avery had scavenged from a store up in Vermont was a particular favorite of her mom's—Not! Avery had glued the sign to the front of her door as a warning to stray visitors.

"It's probably best that I don't look," her mother would say with a sigh, closing the door as quickly as possible.

It didn't help matters that her older brother Scott's bedroom looked like a feature in *Architectural Digest*. He was a neat freak. His room always looked like nobody had been in it for a year. Bed neatly made, everything lined up on his desk in perfect rows, his black-and-white sports photographs matted and framed on the walls, and all in matching black frames.

Next to Scott, Avery felt like an accident waiting to happen. She knew that part of this was because neatness wasn't the biggest priority in her life. What was the point of making her bed when she was only going to get right back into it at night?

Her mother didn't bother Avery too much about keeping her room clean. From time to time, their housekeeper Carla would venture into Avery's room to do some basic straightening up. But Carla wouldn't go into Walter's closet. She was afraid of snakes.

The family also had a gardener who came and tidied up the garden. Her mother had a greenhouse and one of her hobbies was growing rare orchids ("cultivating" was the word she used). Now, what on earth was the point of THAT? Flowers were okay. But growing flowers in pots in a glass room for no good reason ... Avery just didn't get that.

Still, her mom had a heart of gold, even if she cared about things that seemed bizarre to Avery. Her mom loved parties, being involved, and giving back. This meant that she was always inviting people over.

Avery's mother loved to have parties. She had a different group over almost every week. One week it was the gardening club. Another week it was her book club. She was also very involved in fund-raising, which meant hosting big parties (usually catered) that Avery found a little boring. Still, she knew her mom was involved in some really good causes. Avery was very much a "live and let live" kind of girl. Her mom let her run around in her soccer gear, so why shouldn't she let her mom enjoy her fund-raising gigs? Plus her mom had a really good sense of humor and loved cartoons as much as Avery did.

Her father, Jake Madden, was as different from her mother as night from day. Maybe that was the reason that they'd split up. Avery's dad was a laid-back country boy while Elizabeth was a sophisticated city girl. It was a classic case of opposites attract. After college, he'd gone backpacking in Nepal for a year. Then worked for the Peace Corps where he and Elizabeth met. Back in Boston, he'd discovered that a desk job wasn't for him. He decided to move west and start a snowboarding shop. Avery adored her dad. She wished that he lived closer; Colorado felt like a million miles away sometimes. But she and her dad were amazing e-mail companions, and sometimes they chatted as much as six times a day.

No time to e-mail Dad now, though. Avery had to get going. One last check on the guinea pigs first ... she had renamed them already, after her two favorite soccer stars. "Hey, Beckham! Hey, Hamm!" she called to them, sticking her fingers through the wire grid of their cage.

They didn't look so well to her. A little sluggish, actually. Maybe she'd given them a bit too much lettuce. Hamm wasn't that interested, but Beckham ate three leaves. She decided she'd better call Maeve and check in with her.

"No more lettuce," Maeve said. "And no more carrots. Better just stick to the pellets."

Maeve gave Avery another lecture about how finicky guinea pigs can be about what they eat, and Avery swore up and down that she'd stick to the list—only a little shredded lettuce: one piece, not three, and nothing but dried guinea pig food until they were both looking perky again. "I'm going to e-mail you the list of what they can eat and what they can't eat," she said sternly. "And also, I'm sending you the instructions about letting them out of their cage. Promise you'll read it, okay?"

"I promise," Avery said.

Sigh. Avery put Hamm and Beckham back into the cage, giving them each a little wave of encouragement. She hoped they looked perkier soon so she could sneak them some of her mother's fancy Bibb lettuce. Only one piece this time.

જ્જ

On Monday night, Maeve and her mother were making lunches together for the next day. Her mom had the big wall calendar lying on the counter and was sneaking glances at it as she made sandwiches.

Maeve looked at it, too. The box for FRIDAY had a note on it in blue. "Maeve and Sam—to Ross's." She bit her lip. This was probably a good time to talk to her mom about Dillon. All she had to do was explain what had happened. Her mom would know what she should say to her dad so she could go out with Dillon without hurting his feelings.

But she kept having this nagging feeling of guilt. She shouldn't have said yes, not without asking first. Not when it involved going all the way downtown. And not when it involved breaking plans she already had.

Not that she exactly needed permission, of course. She was almost thirteen! That night she went out with Nick ... well, that was different. She'd met him at Montoya's, which was his parents' bakery. And then she'd dragged him over to the Movie House. Her dad and Jimmy, the projectionist, were there the whole time, even if they were in the back of the cinema.

They won't mind, Maeve assured herself. But I should ask them ... just in case ...

❁ 141 ❁

This wasn't a good time, though. Her mother was really distracted. She was doing what she called "multitasking." That meant that she was paying as much attention to the calendar as she was to the lunch preparations. Maeve had to dive in and rescue her lunch before she ended up with Sam's vile robot soup instead of her favorite carrots and dip.

"Shoot. I have two late nights this week," her mother muttered, crossing something out on the calendar and frowning. "I'm going to need to ask Dad to get you at Hebrew School on Tuesday and Thursday."

Maeve brightened. "I could just skip Hebrew School this week," she offered generously.

Her mother frowned at her. "Maeve, just because Dad and I are living in two different places doesn't mean that our standards are changing. We still care about the same things that we always did. Like being on time, and getting assignments done."

And not going to a Celtics game with a guy unless you've asked for permission, Maeve thought uneasily. But she pushed the thought away. They probably wouldn't mind, she assured herself. And they knew Dillon—at least a little. Didn't her dad tell her to take care of herself?

"Okay, Mom," Maeve said cheerfully. "Don't worry, Dad can get me from Hebrew School."

Her mother turned to give her an impulsive hug. "Maeve, you've been such a big help. You have no idea how much it means to me," she said warmly.

The little stab of guilt was getting worse. Maeve bit her lip. Ask her—NOW.

"Um—Mom?" she began.

The phone rang, and her mother glanced at the number

on their caller ID box. "Shoot—it's my boss. I have to take this, Maeve."

Maeve sighed, turning back to finish packing lunches. So much for that. It wasn't like she hadn't tried to ask for permission.

After dinner, Maeve spread her homework out all over the dining room table. She needed to have a draft of interview questions ready for Ms. Rodriguez by tomorrow.

What do I want to know? Maeve thought, opening up her laptop and drumming her fingers on the table.

The thing Maeve MOST wanted to know about was how to grow up. She didn't really know how to put this into words. So, how did you get from being a kid to being a grown-up? How did her parents figure out what kind of things they wanted to do when they grew up? What kind of life they'd want to lead? She'd seen old home movies of her mom when she was a girl. Birthday parties, family vacations ... how did that girl grow up and become her mother?

"Mom!" Maeve called.

Her mother came into the dining room. She looked tired, and she had a pile of work in her arms.

"Mom, I need help. We're doing this big project in English and social studies and we're supposed to find out about our personal history and I'm totally lost," Maeve sighed.

Her mother set her files down on the dining room table. "What sort of things are you writing about?"

"It's up to us. But I need to interview you and Daddy." Maeve sighed. "I'm just not sure what to ASK, that's the problem."

Her mother sat down, lacing her fingers together the way she did when she was thinking. "Did I ever tell you much about your great-grandmother?"

Maeve shook her head. "Was she the one who worked in the hat factory?"

"For a while." Her mother smiled. "But she was also a 'flapper,' she had a raccoon coat and she danced on Broadway for a few years."

Maeve's eyes lit up. "No way!" This might not be as good as being related to Audrey Hepburn, but still. Broadway was Broadway.

"Her name was Sylvie. She was extraordinary." Maeve's mother smiled. "She was only five feet tall, but really gorgeous, and they always let her dance right up in front because she was so tiny. Let me find some pictures of her for you, okay?"

Maeve was thrilled. She had talent in her bones and it dated way back. This project was getting more interesting by the moment.

Maeve tried to type up a few questions about great-grandma Sylvie while her mother went off to look for photographs. She was on question number two when the phone rang.

It was Dillon.

Maeve tried her hardest to sound nonchalant. "Hey," she said, in her most casual I'm-glad-to-hear-from-you-but-this-is-SO-normal voice. "What's up?"

"Nothing much. Just wanted to check in with you," Dillon said. How could he sound so cute and so COOL even over the phone line? "I checked with my dad, and he said we're all set for Friday. We'll pick you up around seven at your place, okay?"

At her place? Here? Maeve's heart skipped a beat. She couldn't think for a second. Great, this was getting more and more confusing by the minute.

"Um ..." Maeve thought fast. "Why don't I just meet you

over at your house?" she shot back. True, her parents probably wouldn't mind her going out with Dillon. But just in case she didn't get around to asking ... they shouldn't meet here. "I've got a class on Friday and I don't really know when it gets out."

Great. Now she was REALLY getting boxed in.

"Okay," Dillon said. "Do you know where I live?"

Maeve wrote down his address and directions. She tried to keep her voice sounding casual. "Dillon—what time do you think we'll be back? Just wondering," she added quickly.

"Probably around ten thirty. Is that okay?" he asked.

Now that, Maeve thought, was the million dollar question. Was that okay? How would she know? Her stomach was in complete knots. Maeve had never, ever done anything like this before. She ALWAYS asked her mom and dad before she went somewhere. It was a Kaplan-Taylor Golden Rule. And now she was breaking it. But she didn't want to seem like a little kid to Dillon. She didn't want him to think she had to ask her parents' permission just to cross the room.

"Oh, that's fine," Maeve said. If she didn't know any better, she would think that absolutely nothing was the matter. She sounded so confident and laid-back. She even chattered for a few minutes with Dillon about their homework assignment and how hard it was. He'd never know that her stomach was churning and churning. And before she'd hung up, they had a plan. Maeve would meet him at his house Friday evening around a quarter to seven.

Now she just had to break the news to her mom and dad.

☙

Maeve closed the door to her bedroom with a sigh. One quick I.M. session with her friends and she was going straight to bed.

She flipped open her laptop. To her surprise, a new screen name was blinking out at her.

It was her father!

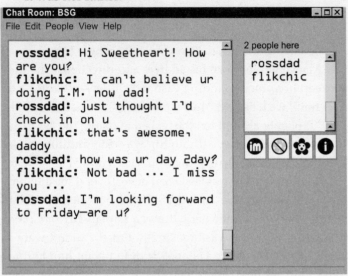

Maeve felt her stomach lurch. Now what? What was she supposed to tell him? That she'd gone ahead and agreed to go to the game with Dillon even though they had plans? And she hadn't even asked him first?

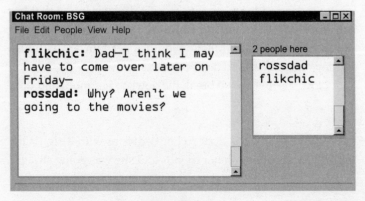

Think, Maeve Kaplan-Taylor. THINK. Maeve bit her lip.

Where were her friends going to be? Could she say she was going to be with them? Maeve remembered: they were sleeping over at Charlotte's house—Katani, Avery, and Isabel. They'd asked her to come and she said she couldn't. Because she had plans with Sam and her Dad.

Maeve wracked her brains.

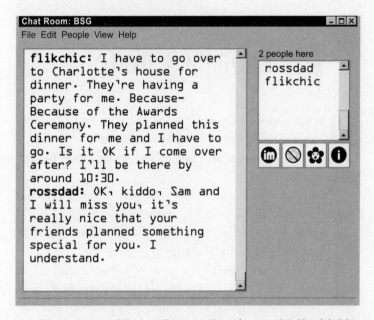

Chat Room: BSG

File Edit People View Help

flikchic: I have to go over to Charlotte's house for dinner. They're having a party for me. Because-Because of the Awards Ceremony. They planned this dinner for me and I have to go. Is it OK if I come over after? I'll be there by around 10:30.
rossdad: OK, kiddo, Sam and I will miss you, it's really nice that your friends planned something special for you. I understand.

2 people here

rossdad
flikchic

Maeve's eyes filled with tears. "I understand." She felt like a worm. A giant worm. Well, it would be okay. She'd do this just this once, and next time she'd ask her parents in the first place and this wouldn't happen again. She promised herself.

And wasn't it worth it, getting to go out with Dillon? Getting to go downtown to a Celtics game, just the two of them? A dream come true!

CHAPTER
15

Promises Made

"Maeve! Avery! Wait up!" Isabel, Katani, and Charlotte were hurrying down the hallway near the seventh-grade lockers, trying to catch Maeve and Avery before English class began.

"Sorry, you people. I was just getting an important lecture on guinea pig food," Avery said.

"I was telling Avery that they have sensitive little digestive tracts," Maeve interrupted.

"Maeve," Charlotte cut in, "we were just talking about the sleepover at my house on Friday night. Are you SURE you can't come? It's not going to be as much fun without you."

Maeve flushed. "I can't," she said, trying to block out the memory of her I.M. session with her father the night before. Friday night was getting more tangled by the minute.

She could tell her friends about Dillon. But that would be even worse, because she'd be asking them to cover for her. She knew that wasn't fair. No, better to keep it all to herself. A secret. She hoped she wouldn't run into Dillon before their date.

Nobody would find out, she assured herself.

"We've got ... plans," she explained. "Anyway, you guys will have fun! And I'll come next time—I promise."

The five girls hurried into Ms. Rodriguez's classroom just before the bell, and Maeve slid into her desk. She was feeling more and more uncomfortable about this whole thing on Friday night. But she couldn't see any way to get out of the mess she was in now. It was too late to ask her parents' permission for something she'd already said yes to. And now that she'd told her dad she had plans with her friends ... well, forget THAT. No, she was just going to have to go through with her plan. Meet Dillon at his house. Go to the game, and get dropped off at her dad's. In all the excitement about their first night there, he'd never focus on who brought her home. She hoped.

Ms. Rodriguez's English class was buzzing. They were all taking the class period to work in small groups on their Heritage Museum reports. *Good*, Maeve thought. She could use some extra class time to work on her project.

Within minutes, everyone had rearranged their desks so they could work with people they knew. Isabel was working with Katani. Avery was working with Charlotte. And Maeve, with just a little bit of maneuvering, managed to pull her desk over so that she could work with Dillon.

He leaned over her desk. "Hey," he said. "I'm really psyched about Friday."

"Me too," Maeve said. She hoped her voice sounded enthusiastic. It wasn't that she wasn't excited anymore. She was. It was just ... well, the whole thing was getting so unbelievably complicated. Maeve could barely remember what she'd told which person about where she was going to be. And she was getting more and more worried that somehow, somebody was going to find out that she was really out with Dillon. She almost didn't want to go now. But, she couldn't say no to Dillon. Especially since his father got the tickets. What a mess!

CR

Avery was up in her bedroom with the door closed tight, lying on her carpet on her stomach. She'd spent the last hour turning her room into a guinea pig Olympics. It took a little ingenuity, but it was totally worth it.

The long jump was the first event. Avery had set up a series of markers so she could measure how far Hamm and Beckham could jump. The high jump was fashioned out of a wire hanger, and she had to admit that neither guinea pig seemed very excited about it.

But she had big hopes for them.

"You guys just need a little exercise—and a little freedom," Avery crooned to them, crawling as fast as she could alongside of Hamm to egg her on as she raced along the side of Avery's bed.

She was pretty certain that with some work, these two could become show guinea pigs. Before the week was out, Avery was sure she'd be able to get them REALLY off and running.

"You're going to be little guinea pig Olympic stars," she told them encouragingly.

A sudden knock on the door made her jump straight up. Oops—it was her mother. She might not be that happy to see these little guys crawling around outside of their cage.

"Avery? Can I come in?"

"Just give me a sec, Mom," Avery said.

She grabbed Hamm and stuffed her back into her cage.

❁ 150 ❁

But where was Beckham, that rascal? She really WAS picking up speed. All that training was paying off. Shoot—now she couldn't seem to find her. Avery stuck her head under her bed skirt, peering around frantically. All she saw was a blue shin guard and a wadded-up pair of sweats. So that's where her shin guard had gone—she'd been searching for it.

"Avery? I need to talk to you," her mother said, sounding a little impatient.

Just as her mother started to turn the door handle, the shin guard started to move across the floor, trailing a sock and a dust ball behind. Beckham! Avery grabbed the shin guard, the sock, and Beckham (who now looked like a dust ball herself) and shoved her quickly into the cage, forgetting to close the lid just as her mother came into the room.

"What's going on in there?" her mother demanded.

"It's messy, Ma. Super, super, SUPER messy. An Olympic-sized mess," Avery informed her—and actually, this was all pretty much true. She didn't want her mother to know that the guinea pigs had been running around. That wasn't part of the deal.

"It is!" her mother said, looking unsettled. "Avery, I really wish you would try to be a little neater. You're old enough now ..." She paused. "But—that isn't really what I came in to talk about. I wanted to let you know that we're all set for Saturday. Mr. Jameson is SO happy that you're going to be here. And that your friends are coming, too."

Avery clapped her hand to her forehead. She'd forgotten all about the dinner on Saturday night. She'd better move fast to round up Katani, Maeve, Isabel, and Charlotte and get them to come over. Not to mention telling them that they were supposed to be showing all those Talbot Academy guests what "girls of today" were really like.

"Okay, Mom. I'll remind everyone," Avery said, trying not to let her mother back in the room. It was hard, because her mother kept pushing the door open a little, and Avery kept trying valiantly to keep it closed.

"And I'll clean my room," Avery said. "I promise I'll have it all cleaned up by Saturday."

"That would be lovely," Avery's mother said, truly pleased. "I appreciate you making the effort, Avery."

It was no small thing to clean her room, but Avery found she wanted to do it. Partly because her mom had been so nice about letting the guinea pigs stay. And partly because it was beginning to be a nightmare. She would clean her room and she would clean the guinea pigs' cage, too. She had until Saturday. It was possible.

CR

After school, Katani knocked lightly on the door to the principal's office.

"Come in!"

Mrs. Fields, her grandmother, always looked so different to Katani here in her office. Maybe it was the little sign that said "Principal" on the door. Maybe it was the stacks of papers and files on her big desk, or the plaques and certificates lining the wall. She just looked so official. Katani was extremely proud of her grandmother. She had so much dignity and presence—she held herself so tall, and her voice always filled the room with firm authority when she spoke at assemblies. If she'd worried at all about what it would be like starting junior high and having her grandmother as the principal, she didn't worry anymore.

"Katani! What brings you here this afternoon?" Her grandmother beamed at her, getting up from her desk and clearing some files off a chair so that Katani could sit down.

Katani set her backpack on the ground. "Well, we're doing a research project in social studies and English, and I wanted to interview you," she said.

Mrs. Fields welcomed her with a big smile.

Katani started to explain, and her grandmother nodded. "Yes. I've heard quite a bit about this project. And I think it's a wonderful idea. Katani, I'm flattered that you'd like to talk with me. Let me just tell Ms. Sahni that I'll be busy for a while, and you and I can talk."

While her grandmother buzzed out to the front office, Katani looked admiringly at the row of quotations above her grandmother's desk. She loved the quotes from Martin Luther King, Jr., but her favorite was from Maya Angelou: "A bird does not sing because it has an answer. It sings because it has a song." She got her notebook out and wrote the quotation down. Her grandmother had chosen all the quotes, and Katani thought that they were great examples of what she admired most in her—her sense of purpose and her understanding of human nature.

"Okay," Mrs. Fields said, turning back to Katani with a smile. "So what can I tell you that you don't already know about me?'

"Well ..." Katani chewed on the end of her pen. "I'm really curious what made you decide to go into education. And also, what it was like being African American here in Brookline in the 1960s?"

Her grandmother nodded. "Those are good questions, Katani. I really did get to see some amazing changes in this city. One of the most rewarding experiences for me was watching the struggle in the African American community to desegregate the schools."

"Were you a part of that?" Katani asked, getting interested. She knew less than she'd like to about what schools had been like in Boston when her grandmother was growing up, and suddenly Katani realized that this would be a great subject to focus on for her part of the Heritage Museum.

"My mother was a teacher. Did you know that? And your great-grandfather was one of the best barbers and hair stylists in Boston." Mrs. Fields sighed. "They died before you were born. But they were amazing people—always fighting for what they believed in. They were both a part of a group called Operation Exodus—a group of African American parents who worked very hard in the '60s to make schools a better place for their children." She looked misty-eyed. "Katani, I would've loved for you to have met them. Both of my parents gave me such a love of education that I always vowed that one day I would become a teacher. And then I became very interested in how schools ran, and before I knew it ... I became a principal!"

"Grandma, you've given me a wonderful idea," Katani said, jumping up to give her a hug. "I know exactly what I want to do my research on now! Thank you so much!"

Mrs. Fields smiled fondly at her, but Katani could tell she was still half-remembering all of the things that were coming back to her. And Katani wanted to learn more about them, too. She was off to the library, ready to put her grandmother's history in context.

Chat Room: BSG

File Edit People View Help

4kicks: u guys I need to ask u a BIG favor
lafrida: what's up
flikchic: yeah what is it
4kicks: my mom's having some important guy over 4 dinner Saturday nite & she needs me to bring ALL of u
Kgirl: y?
skywriter: whats the dinner 4?
4kicks: some fundraiser for that girls school she used 2 go 2
skywriter: why does she want us there?
Kgirl: who cares y—bet there'll be great food! count me in—
4kicks: i'll owe you guys forever if you come
skywriter: OK
flikchic: OK
lafrida: ditto
4kicks: u guys r the best. 0 he wants to know what girls 2day are like
lafrida: we'll show him
skywriter: right! we'll be there!

5 people here

4kicks
lafrida
flikchic
Kgirl
skywriter

CHAPTER

16

Lost and Found

Wednesday afternoon, there was the usual crush at the seventh-grade lockers. Avery was digging through the mess at the bottom of hers, trying to find her soccer cleats, when Maeve came hurrying up.

"I've been looking for you," she said, panting a little. "I wanted to check and see how my babies are. You didn't say a word about them today!"

Avery bit her lip. She didn't think this was the best time to tell Maeve that one of her "babies" was AWOL: "absent without leave." She had forgotten to secure the lid on the cage when her mother had come in the room. Avery had combed her bedroom last night, but she couldn't find a single sign of Beckham. Hamm was sleeping peacefully in her cage, apparently enjoying having the whole space to herself. But where was Beckham?

Avery had looked absolutely everywhere. Under the bed, under her desk, behind the bureau ... a wave of panic had washed over her when she realized that the door to her bathroom was open, and maybe Beckham had gotten herself into a jam. She'd peered frantically down into the toilet, but thank heavens, she wasn't in there. And not in the sink or shower, either. So then where could she be?

Finally, she'd had no choice but to go to bed, vowing to get up early and search all over again. Surely Beckham would show up in the morning.

Well, guess what? Morning had come, and still no Beckham. Even worse, Hamm was looking kind of glum. She seemed to sense that her buddy was free and she was still trapped in this cage. "Don't YOU get out, too," Avery scolded her, but then she felt so guilty that she gave her some extra guinea pig food. Having guinea pigs was a lot more complicated than she'd imagined.

Now what was she supposed to tell Maeve? That she'd been so irresponsible that one of her little guys was loose somewhere in Avery's house?

"Um—Maeve—I am SO LATE for soccer," Avery gasped, and before Maeve could say anything else, she'd jumped on her skateboard and taken off.

Weird, Maeve thought, staring after her with a confused look on her face. And she'd been about to give Avery an important warning about Ben, the bigger of her two guinea pigs. She wanted to let Avery know that Ben was an unbelievable escape artist, and that Avery should guard the door if she let Ben out of the cage ... even for a second. Once Ben had gotten loose and Maeve hadn't been able to find her for almost a week.

Oh well, Maeve thought. Avery must know what she was doing. Anyway, Dillon was heading over ... she better get out of here before he said something about Friday in front of her friends.

"Hey," Dillon said, falling into step beside her. "You still psyched for Friday night?"

Maeve gulped. "Uh—yeah. Yes. I mean, I am," she said, the words stumbling out in a rush.

Dillon started filling her in on one of the Celtics' forwards. He was still injured and it wasn't clear if he could play or not. "It should be a great game," Dillon said. He glanced at her. "Maeve, I really feel bad about you having to walk over to my house. Why won't you let my dad and me pick you up at your place? We can be there around six. It's right on our way," he added.

"NO!" Maeve said. It came out much more emphatically than she'd meant it to and she turned red. "I mean, that is SO sweet of you," she said, struggling to think of a good reason why Dillon shouldn't come and get her.

How's this, she thought. My dad is supposed to be coming over to pick up Sam and me right around six o'clock. How am I going to explain it to him if Dillon and his dad show up at the same time? Especially since I'm supposed to be on my way over to my friends' house for a celebration dinner in my honor?

"But you know ... I'm going to be out anyway ... right near your house," she said weakly. "Seriously. Just—don't worry about it."

She barely gave Dillon a chance to answer. Just a quick wave and she dashed off, furious with herself for having gotten into this mess in the first place.

Why hadn't she just asked her parents? Why had she let everything get so ridiculously complicated for no good reason?

ଔ

After school, Avery hunted absolutely everywhere for Beckham, but there was no sign of her.

"This is hopeless," she told herself, shaking her head.

Her mom called upstairs to her. "Avery! Dinner's going to be ready in twenty minutes. It's just you and me tonight—Scott's at Chess Club."

"Okay," Avery hollered back.

She looked out the window, a frown on her face. What could be worse? Beckham was probably lost forever. And on top of that, she still had her Heritage Museum report to work on tonight.

Avery's eye fell on the carriage house across the garden. Could Beckham have gotten out somehow? Suppose she'd gotten outside ... suppose Carla had opened the door and she ran out into the garden.

She sure hoped not. But on a whim, Avery decided to go out and search. And she'd better do it now, before the light faded.

No sign of Beckham in the garden. Avery used a flashlight to shine in and around all of the bushes, but no luck. And no sign of her in the carriage house, either. Avery looked behind the trash cans, the coils of garden hose ... everywhere she could think of. She even climbed up the ladder to shine her flashlight around in the loft. But it was hopeless. No Beckham.

She was about to shimmy back down the ladder when her flashlight fell on a box against the far wall marked "AVERY ☺ " It was next to a bunch of other boxes, right near the one marked Talbot Academy. Avery was surprised that she hadn't seen it the last time she was up here, helping her mother look for her old yearbooks.

She still had a few minutes before dinner. Avery couldn't help herself. She had to check out the box and see what was inside.

The box smelled faintly damp, but everything inside was

carefully wrapped in plastic. It seemed to be mostly manila file folders—tons and tons of paperwork. Avery was about to close the lid when she saw something colorful in the bottom of the box. Also wrapped in plastic, it looked like a quilt—but the fabrics didn't look like quilting fabrics. They actually looked Korean.

In fact, as Avery started to rifle through the folders, it became clear that this whole box was filled with material having to do with her adoption. Papers from the adoption agency in Seoul, Korea. Papers from an agency in New York. Document after document, a huge fat file called "Home Study 1990–1991." A map of Korea. Several books on adoption. Avery kept rifling through the box, hoping to find ...

What?

She wasn't sure. Something. A photograph? A tape? Some sort of evidence of the place that she'd come from. But all she could find was paperwork. It all looked pretty boring. The only other thing was the cloth that looked like a quilt, but wasn't.

Avery carefully lifted the cloth, still in its plastic cocoon, and brought it back down the ladder with her. She'd go and ask her mother about it—Avery was sure she'd know what it was.

☙

"Mom, what's this?" Avery asked, coming into the kitchen a few minutes later and handing the cloth to her mother.

An expression of recognition came over her face, and then pleasure. "Where did you find this?" she asked, looking delighted. "I've been looking all over for it, but I couldn't remember where I put it."

"In a box up in the loft," Avery said.

"The loft ..." her mother still looked puzzled.

Avery thought fast. She didn't want to tell her mother that Beckham was lost. "I'm doing this Heritage Museum project for school," she said, "and remember, when I was up there helping you look for yearbooks, I thought there might be some cool stuff I could find to bring in. And I found this box up there with my name on it."

"So THAT'S where I put it. I'm so glad you found it. I thought I had put it with your baby clothes," her mother exclaimed.

"What is it?" Avery demanded, getting more and more curious.

"It's a *bojagi*. A carrying cloth," her mother said, carefully taking out the cloth and turning it over and over in her hands. "Avery, when we adopted you, the agency gave this to us. It came from your birth mother. It's a traditional cloth from Korea, used to carry things ... See, you fold it up, and the things you carry—well, they give the cloth its shape."

Avery took the cloth back, staring at it. "So this came with me?" she asked wonderingly.

Her mother nodded. "I wanted you to have it for your thirteenth birthday. But you know," she said, leaning over to give Avery a hug, "I'm actually glad that you found it yourself. Somehow that seems even more fitting. Now, there's something else I want you to have. I wrote a letter to you on the first night you joined our family. I think maybe this would be the right time for you to read it."

Avery's mother left the room and came back a minute later with a small baby pillow, which she handed to Avery. There was a note sticking out of a pocket in the pillow. Avery opened the note, which smelled a bit like sweet lemonade, and read:

My dearest baby girl:

To finally have you in my arms is a joy that is beyond my ability to describe. What does one say when someone puts a daughter in your arms for the first time? Does one whisper in her daughter's ear that she is loved as much as the tallest mountain? Does one wish for all the happiness in the world for her precious little girl? Does a mother tell her daughter that she will always be her daughter and always have arms to hold her? Does her mother shout that her girl is the most wonderful, beautiful little girl in the world? Yes, my dearest little Avery Koh Madden, your mother does all of that. And she says softly, welcome to my heart, little one. You will always have a safe haven with me.

Love forever and a universe,
Your mother,
Elizabeth Madden

(I hope you like pink, but it's just fine if you don't. I want you to be whoever you want to be. Always remember that.)

भ

When she finished, Avery looked up and her mother held open her arms. Wordlessly, Avery moved toward her. Mother and daughter held on to each other for several quiet minutes.

Later in her bedroom, Avery traced the pattern on the bojagi with her finger. She had grown up so comfortable with the idea of being adopted that she often didn't think about it. And then, at moments like this, it flew out at her. How she had two worlds that she belonged to, one that she knew so well, and one that lay in her past. She and her dad had talked for years about going to Korea together one day. Avery really wanted to do that. Looking at this cloth, Avery felt a sudden, intense longing to learn more about her background. Her mother was right. It was important that Avery had found this herself. She knew that this was a definite choice to show the class for her part of the Heritage Museum. But first, she needed to do some research.

Avery's Blog

My Top Five Ever Most Annoying Questions
and Comments About Being Adopted:
1. Who are your REAL parents? Are they
   Korean?
   Answer: My real parents are the people
   who've loved me and raised me since I
   was four months old. Elizabeth and
   Jake Madden, aka Mom and Dad. And they
   hate this question too. They happen to
   be divorced but they still love me
   like crazy. If you want to know about
   my BIRTH parents, well, I don't know
   who they are. Maybe one day I'll find
   out, but for now it's enough that I
   know that they lived in a village
   outside of Seoul and that they needed
   to give me up for adoption.
2. You're such a lucky girl!
   Answer: I guess I am, but not for the
   reasons that you think. The way you
   say that sounds INSULTING. (My parents
   say that THEY'RE the lucky ones. I

think we're lucky to have each other.
Period.)
3. Where are you from?
Answer: Brookline, Massachusetts.
(This always gets stares. Not the
answer that they want.)
4. Where are you REALLY from?
Brookline, Massachusetts. But my dad
lives in Aspen, Colorado. (I know, I
know. But I'm not going to give in and
tell them I'm REALLY from Korea. 'Cause
the truth is, I AM from here. I've
lived here almost thirteen years.
Pretty much my entire life, minus the
first four months.)
5. Oooh ... you're so good at (fill in
the blank—soccer, math, whatever). Do
you think maybe that's genetic?
Answer: I haven't figured this one
out. What I'd LIKE to say is: "Do you
think rude questions are genetic?" But
I don't.

Here's what people DON'T ask and
what I can't answer, either. How is
being adopted important? Or different?
Is it a part of what makes me AVERY?
I don't know the answer to this. I
just don't. But sometimes I really
wish I did.

ଔ

That night Avery slept with the bojagi spread out on the pillow beside her. It was beautiful. She loved tracing the patterns on the cloth with her fingers. And just before she fell asleep, an amazing feeling of calm came over her. And a phrase floated into her head, a phrase her mother had used.

The shape of what it carries.

She wasn't sure why that phrase was so soothing, but saying it over and over to herself, she fell into a deep, restful sleep.

CHAPTER
17

Bad Move

Avery was trying to explain what a *bojagi* was at lunch on Friday. "Just picture a quilt, but smaller. Mine, well, it's really beautiful," Avery said. "It's unique. I've never seen anything like it before."

Katani, who loved fabric of every kind, couldn't wait to see it. "I like the idea of carrying things in a cloth," she said. She looked with interest at Avery. "You know, this may be the first time I've heard you use the word 'beautiful' to describe something other than a soccer play, Avery Madden."

Avery laughed. "I'm not THAT blind to culture, Katani. It's just—" She shrugged. "I don't know. I think I can really connect to this, partly because of where it comes from. I guess I just like this Heritage Project more than I thought I would."

"Me, too," Katani admitted. "I'm doing my research on schools—I got the idea from my grandmother. And you know what I found out? There was a school for African Americans that started in Boston in 1835!"

"Wow," Avery said admiringly. The two of them started

trading research tips, and soon Charlotte joined in on the comparative strengths of using the library versus the Internet.

Maeve was distracted, but her friends gave each other knowing glances. They were all certain it was because tonight was the night—her first time spending the night at her dad's.

"Don't worry, Maeve," Isabel said, leaning over and giving her arm a squeeze. "I bet it'll go better than you think it will."

Maeve sat up straight, looking completely embarrassed. How did Isabel guess what she was thinking? Two completely different scenes were running through her mind. In one, she and Dillon were sitting arm in arm, watching the Celtics. Of course, in Maeve's imagination, the Fleet Center was all soft-focus and dimly lit ... more like Lincoln Center than a sweaty basketball court ... and Dillon was leaning in to kiss her ...

Yikes. In the other scenario, Maeve saw herself cowering against Dillon, with an angry stampede of people stomping up to them, demanding to know what she was doing here. Her mom. Her dad. Sam. All three of them stomping up on one side, shouting at her. And on the other side her four best friends ... She could just hear them yelling. "You didn't tell us your parents were splitting up! Now you go out with Dillon and you don't tell us what's going on, AGAIN—"

"Maeve," Katani said, turning to inspect her tray. "You haven't eaten your Tuna Surprise." The affection and humor in her voice were mixed with a trace of concern. "Are you Okay?"

Maeve nodded. "Just ... fine," she said.

The girls went back to chattering about the plans for the weekend, and the sleepover that night at Charlotte's and what movie to rent. And the dinner party the next night at Avery's.

"I guess I'll see you guys tomorrow night," Maeve said, trying to sound casual as she picked up her tray.

Everyone wished her luck on her first weekend at her dad's, and Maeve felt that familiar twinge of guilt again. Her friends were the best. She felt like she didn't deserve them. But maybe she'd be lucky and this whole thing would work out Okay and she would never get something so mixed-up again ... ever.

CR

Getting ready for their first weekend away at Dad's was harder than Maeve expected—harder logistically, and harder emotionally. Her mom was there to help them pack, and Maeve could tell that it wasn't exactly easy for her, either. Much as Mom was trying to be upbeat, Maeve could see that her eyes kept getting watery.

Sam was taking it pretty hard. He packed and unpacked his camouflage duffel about fifteen times. He had to have just the right toothpaste—this gross blue goop with glitter in it. And his favorite blue blanket, which was worn to bits and looked like a giant fleece rag. Then came Sam's most precious possession—and his deepest, darkest secret. He had a rubber action toy that he called "Captain Mike," which he slept with every night. And he had to pack Mike along with his blanket and his two pair of grubby corduroy pants, his whole wardrobe, as far as Maeve could tell.

"Sam, quit repacking! You're going to lose something," she told him after he'd checked and rechecked the contents of his bag for the tenth time.

Maeve herself was in quite a state. On the one hand, she had to pack for the weekend herself. It was harder than she'd imagined, figuring out everything she needed to take with her. Homework ... day planner ... hair dryer ... laptop ... two of her latest magazines ... and then on top of that, what to wear? She had this dinner tomorrow night at Avery's. That meant something kind of dressy. Her pajamas ... something comfy to hang out at Dad's ... and what if she went out with her friends on Sunday?

"Maeve, you can't bring all that," Sam gasped. "It's gonna fill up Dad's whole apartment!"

Maeve glared at him. Right now she didn't want to remember that she had to share a room with Sam this whole weekend. She stuffed in her two favorite hairbrushes and her shampoo bag—Maeve was a shampoo fanatic—and stood back, trying to think what she might have forgotten.

Of course in the midst of all of this, she was supposed to be getting ready to go out with Dillon. Try doing THAT with a nosy little brother getting in your way.

"Why do you have to wear PERFUME," he grumbled, "if you're just going to a dumb old dinner with your friends?"

Maeve was trying to brush perfume into her hair the way she'd read in the "How to Stay on His Mind" column in *Seventeen* magazine. She tried to ignore Sam and keep her eye on her watch.

It was almost five. She stuffed another sweater into her duffel and lugged it into the hallway. "Sam, be sure Dad picks this up when he gets you, okay? I need all of this stuff for the weekend."

Sam was looking forlornly at his room, which looked a little empty without his blanket and Captain Mike.

Maeve stooped down and gave him a hug. "It's going to be okay," she whispered to Sam and herself. "Honest, Sam. It won't be that bad."

Maeve felt a sudden rush of tenderness for her younger brother. How do you explain to an eight-year-old that moving back and forth from one house to another probably gets easier with time?

"I don't think ..." Sam whispered, his voice breaking a little, "that Captain Mike is going to like this. He'd rather just stay here."

Maeve hugged him harder. "As long as he's with you, he's going to be fine," she told him firmly.

She'd done her best to comfort him. Now she'd better get going if she wanted to make it over to Dillon's house in time. Dillon's house was three stops away on the trolley and she didn't want to be late.

ॐ

"You must be Maeve. I'm Dennis, Dillon's dad."

Maeve had to hide a smile—Dillon's father looked so much like Dillon. He seemed to have the same easygoing, affable character, too. It was easy to talk to him.

It turned out that Dillon's dad wasn't just driving them to the game—he was staying and watching it, too. Same with Dillon's older brother Gabe. Maeve wasn't sure whether she was glad about that or not. It was definitely a little less romantic than if it had just been the two of them. But by this point she was so relieved to have made it safely over to Dillon's without being found out that she was just happy, that was all. And it was fun watching the game with Dillon. Before they got into the car to drive downtown, Maeve turned her cell phone to vibrate. She didn't want anyone bothering them during the game.

The first half passed in a blur. Dillon kept telling her things about the players and cracking jokes, and it felt like the night was just flying by. Maeve wished it would slow down. She LOVED being here, sitting really close to Dillon. She kept noticing that his hand was inching closer and closer to hers. Was he trying to hold hands, or was it just an accident? She couldn't tell.

Well, they still had halftime, and the whole second half. Maeve was having the time of her life. She just wanted this to last forever.

CR

Sam and Ross got back from the movie at around nine o'clock. At first it was fun getting to explore the apartment again, and Dad made Sam a microwave s'more—Sam's favorite "sandwich." But when bedtime finally came, Sam started to get tearful. He missed Mom. And he missed Maeve.

"She'll be back soon. Don't worry," Dad said, giving him a hug. "She's just nearby at Charlotte's. She should be here in about an hour or so. Let's get you unpacked and ready for sleep—okay?"

Sammy nodded. He dragged his camouflage duffel into the little bedroom and began taking things out, one at a time. His blanket he spread out neatly on the lower bunk. Maeve could take the top one tonight. Then his *Star Wars* toothpaste. He even laid his clothes out for the morning.

But where was Captain Mike?

Sam's lip started to wobble. He looked everywhere. He shook the duffel out—but no Mike. He crawled under the bed—still no Mike. He even shook out the legs of his brown corduroy pants, but he couldn't find Mike ANYWHERE. He started to cry in earnest.

"We'll find him. Don't worry," his father said, hugging

❁ 171 ❁

him tightly. "Let's call Mom and see if he fell out while you were packing."

Sam nodded, sniffling. But when they called home, there was no answer. Instead, his mother's voice on the answering machine greeted them, brightly inviting them to leave a message. And when they tried her cell phone, there was no answer, either.

"She must be out," Sam's dad said. He glanced down at Sam and seemed to make a decision. "Let's try Maeve over at Charlotte's. She may know where Captain Mike is."

Sam brightened up. He was dying to talk to Maeve anyway. Maybe she'd come over NOW if she knew how sad he was.

"Okay, buster. If I get you the number, why don't you call?" Sam's dad said, passing him the cordless phone.

Charlotte was in the middle of trying to recreate her chocolate fondue recipe when the telephone rang.

"Katani—can you get it?" Charlotte called. "I've got chocolate all over my hands."

Katani nodded, diving for the phone.

"Hey," someone said, in a squeaky little voice. "This is Sam Kaplan-Taylor?" The way Sam talked, it always sounded like he was making sentences into questions. "Can I talk to Maeve?"

Katani blinked. "She's—" She paused. Wait a second. Wasn't Maeve with HIM?

"Uh, she isn't here," Katani said. She was briefly unsettled, then decided that this was what she and Maeve sometimes called a "Sam Moment."

Dead silence. Then a funny little muffled sound. Then: "She ISN'T? Then where IS she?"

Katani thought about this. "Hang on a second, Sam." She covered the phone with her hand, looking around at her friends. "It's Sam. He wants to know where Maeve is."

"Isn't she with him?" Charlotte asked, licking chocolate off a wooden spoon.

"Yeah, I thought that's why she isn't HERE," Isabel said. "She's supposed to be out with Sam and her dad."

The girls exchanged glances. Katani was still holding the phone to her ear.

An instant later, Sam was gone and Maeve's dad was on the line. His voice sounded worried. "Sam tells me that Maeve isn't there," he said. "Who's this—is this Charlotte?"

"No," Katani said, gulping. "It's Katani." She glanced uneasily at her friends. "Um—we kind of thought ... well, we thought Maeve was going out with YOU tonight."

"I see," Maeve's father said shortly. He didn't sound happy. "Thank you, Katani."

He sounded like he was about to hang up.

"Wait!" Katani cried. "If she isn't with you, and she isn't with us—then where is she?"

"That," Maeve's father said sternly, "is exactly what I want to know."

He hung up, and Katani was left staring helplessly at her friends.

"It's Maeve," she said simply, as they all stared at her. "She's missing."

They stared at each other. Where on earth could Maeve be? What if something had happened to her, or she was in some kind of trouble?

CHAPTER
18

Busted

Maeve had her arm through Dillon's, eyes glued to the second half of the game. The Celtics were up by six points, and the excitement in the Garden was building. She still couldn't believe this was happening—it was all like a dream. Sitting so close to Dillon ... the brilliant colors and energy on the court ... the heady applause ... it was incredibly fun. She didn't ever want the game to stop.

She was just wriggling over a TINY bit closer to Dillon when she felt her phone vibrate in the pocket of her jacket— right between Dillon's side and hers. He could probably feel it too. She tried pulling away a little bit, but there it went again. Buzzing against her side—and Dillon's—over and over again.

"What's that?" Dillon asked, surprised.

Shoot. Maeve did NOT want to answer her phone.

"Oh—nothing," she said, trying to brush it off with an airy little wave of her hand. But there it went again. And she should've known better. Dillon was Mr. Cell Phone. He knew every last detail about the latest technology and of course he realized right away that it was her phone buzzing away like that!

"It's your phone," he told her. "Want to answer it?"

Maeve couldn't think of a good reason to say no. "Sure," she said uneasily, sliding the phone out and feeling it buzzing away in her hand like it was alive. She popped it open and saw her Dad's new number appear on the screen.

NO, Maeve thought. This couldn't be happening.

She looked around her in horror. How was she going to disguise the roaring applause all around her? There was no way her father was going to mistake the noise all around her for the sound of five girls having a sleepover at Charlotte's house.

Unless she scooted out of the bleachers and made her way to someplace quiet.

"Dillon, I better answer this outside. I'll be right back," she said, snapping the phone shut.

She had to say "excuse me" to dozens of people, most of them looking a little irritated as she made her way through the crowded row and out to the stairs. She raced out to the concession stands, heart pounding, and quickly called her father back. PHEW. It was much quieter out here. Maybe she could pull this off.

"MAEVE," her father said. His voice sounded funny. Not exactly happy with her. "Do you mind telling me where on earth you are?"

Maeve bit her lip and wound a strand of red hair around one finger. This was a tough one. Did he know where she was—or where she WASN'T? She couldn't tell from his voice. She had a horrible choice to make. She could confess right away—but then what if he didn't actually know she wasn't at Charlotte's? Or she could keep up the lie. But then—

She didn't even seem to make the choice consciously. The lie just jumped out of her mouth, like all the ones before it. It was like once this whole thing got rolling, she couldn't find her center anymore. It was like she was in a play and someone was feeding her lines. "I told you," she said weakly, hoping against hope that he hadn't somehow found out this wasn't true. "Remember? Charlotte's having a sleepover, and—"

"Maeve!" her father broke in, sparing her any further attempts to dig the hole she was in even deeper. "I already called Charlotte's house. They thought you were with ME."

Maeve felt like all the air had been sucked out of her body. "Oh," she said in a tiny voice. "They did?"

"Yes, Maeve, they did." Her father was clearly hopping mad. "And I thought you were with them. And do you know WHY we all thought that?"

"Because ..." Maeve glanced around her, hoping no one was listening. Fortunately the couple nearby seemed focused on buying refreshments. "I guess because I told you that," she said weakly.

She was definitely caught. No doubt about it.

"So let me just repeat my question, Maeve. Where EXACTLY are you?"

"I'm at the Garden," Maeve whispered. "With Dillon Johnson and his dad. Watching the Celtics game."

This was greeted with complete and utter silence. Not a word.

Say something, Maeve thought. Don't make me suffer! Yell at me or tell me that I shouldn't have lied—just say SOMETHING. It was just too painful to listen to the shocked silence on the other end of the line.

"I see," her father said at last. Very quietly.

"Daddy, I was going to tell you ... I mean, ask you," Maeve blurted out. "I swear! It just all got so confusing. I was afraid of hurting your feelings since we had plans for tonight ... and then I kind of told Dillon yes and I didn't want you to be mad at me for saying yes without asking first ... and then one thing led to another and the next thing I knew I started covering it up ... it seemed to take on a life of its own and I just couldn't stop. I'm so sorry."

"I think," her father said finally, "that we're going to talk about this when you get home, Maeve. Would you mind telling me when that's going to be?"

"Ten thirty," Maeve whispered. "The game's almost over, Daddy."

"I'll be waiting," her father said shortly. "And Maeve—"

"Yes?" Maeve's mouth felt dry.

"Please call your friends and let them know that you're Okay. They're all frantic about where you are."

Maeve hit speed dial #4 on her cell phone, leaning back against the wall near the concession stand. Dillon was going to think she'd died out here, which come to think of it, wasn't that far from the truth. She probably WOULD be dead once her parents were through with her. Not to mention her friends. How was she going to explain this to them?

She could hear the crowd cheering wildly inside. Someone had scored for the Celtics.

"Maeve? Where ARE you?" Charlotte cried.

Maeve could hear her calling out to the others. "It's Maeve! She's okay, wherever she is."

"Charlotte," Maeve said miserably. This was even worse than talking to her dad. "I'm kind of ... this is really confusing, but I'm actually downtown." She paused. "With Dillon." She paused again. "At the basketball game. The Celtics."

❖ 177 ❖

Charlotte was quiet for a minute. "But why? I don't get it," she said.

That was Charlotte, Maeve thought. So loyal and kind. She would NEVER fib to one of her friends.

"Why didn't you tell us you were going with Dillon to the game?"

"I didn't tell you," Maeve said in a low voice, "because I didn't want you to have to cover for me if my dad called. Everything got so mixed up. I'm SO SO sorry. I didn't mean any of this. I wish it all hadn't happened, but it's too late ..."

Maeve could hear Charlotte reporting this back to Isabel, Avery, and Katani. The next thing she knew, Avery had grabbed the phone. Typical Avery. She wanted to know what the score was.

Katani grabbed it next. Katani sometimes had a quick temper, and this was the sort of thing that really got her upset. "Maeve, are you out of your mind? Your dad was really worried ... *we* were worried. You told us you were going with your dad and Sam!"

Maeve tried to muddle through her apology again, but Katani was having none of it. "You didn't tell us your parents were separating. And now this. *What* is going on?"

Maeve sniffled. Her eyes were filling with tears. "I'm SORRY," she cried. "I said I was sorry."

"Isabel wants to talk to you," Katani said abruptly.

Yikes, Maeve thought.

Isabel's voice sounded despondent. "Maeve, are you mad at us? Don't you trust us anymore?" she asked plain-tively.

Things were getting worse and worse and worse. Maeve just couldn't see how to make them understand. She hadn't intended it to be this way. She'd made one mistake, and then tried to fix it by covering it up, and the next thing she knew, everything had snowballed. Everyone she cared about was mad and disappointed. And now she was going to have to fake her way through the rest of the evening. Either that, or she was going to have to tell Dillon the truth.

CR

Dillon stared at her. "Now? You want to leave NOW?"

The game was tied, 86–86. The crowd was insane with excitement. It was the end of the third quarter, and people were stamping their feet and shouting as the players moved deftly from one side of the court to the other.

Maeve's eyes filled with tears. "I have to, Dillon. I did something wrong, and I have to go home … I have to go home NOW!" In a whisper, she haltingly tried to explain to Dillon what had happened. His eyes got bigger and bigger. This was the most embarrassing moment of her life.

"Okay," he said at last with a sigh. "Let me tell my dad."

He leaned over and tapped his father on the shoulder. It took two attempts to get his father to drag his attention away from the court. Maeve thought that everyone in the entire arena could hear his father's expression of utter disbelief when Dillon repeated what Maeve had said—that she needed to go home. NOW.

This time, the "excuse me's" didn't meet with much enthusiasm from their neighbors in the stands. People wanted to watch the game, and they were annoyed with the disruption. Dillon wasn't saying a word, and Dillon's father— well, it was hard to describe the expression on his face. Maeve had a feeling that she wasn't going to be the most popular person in the Johnson household for a while. Gabe was almost purple, he was so upset.

The more she apologized, the worse it got. Finally, she just stopped. The car ride home was interminable. Dillon's father kept trying to find a radio station broadcasting the game. The back of his neck was turning a dull red, which Maeve thought probably wasn't a good sign. Gabe didn't say a single word.

This was not the way Maeve had pictured their evening ending. By the time they got to her dad's place in Washington Square, no one was saying a word.

"I'm so sorry—" Maeve tried for the hundredth time to apologize.

But Dillon just shook his head. "Don't worry," he whispered. "My dad won't stay mad for long. But I think I better go calm him down, Maeve. He's kind of a freak when it comes to basketball."

Maeve felt like her face was the color of a tomato when she said good-night to Mr. Johnson. There really wasn't any point in apologizing one more time. Something told her that she'd better save that for her OWN dad.

Maeve opened the door to her father's apartment, her heart pounding. She had no idea what her father was going to say. She'd made mistakes before, but never one this big.

She could hear voices. Her father's—and her mother's.

What was her mom doing here?

She didn't have long to wonder.

"Maeve!" Sam yelled. "You are in SO MUCH TROUBLE!"

"That's enough, Sam," her mother said. She was standing near Maeve's father in the galley kitchen, her arms crossed. Definitely not looking happy.

Maeve swallowed. "Mom," she said weakly. "Why are you here? Did Dad tell you—"

Her mother and father glanced at each other. Their expressions were hard to read. It was clear that they were both angry, but more than that, they seemed disappointed. Really disappointed.

"Mom and Dad," Maeve gulped. "I am SO SORRY. I don't know how this all even happened. I know I should've asked you guys before I went out with Dillon. But one thing just kind of led to another ... and before I knew it ..."

"Maeve," her mother said in a low voice. "You've broken our trust. More than that, you've let down your father—and your brother. Tonight was a big night for them. They were counting on you."

Maeve hung her head miserably, her eyes brimming with tears.

Her father paced back and forth, massaging his hands. Maeve didn't think she'd ever seen him look this angry and upset.

"Maeve, we were out of our minds with worry. Before we found out where you were—we were frantic. Boston is a big city. Anything could've happened to you!"

Her mother nodded vehemently. "When I got those messages on my cell phone—Maeve. I came racing over here—I didn't know WHAT to think."

"We can't let this go," her father added. "Maeve, we've given you a great deal of freedom because you've always earned it. Well, that trust has been broken now. You're going to need to earn it back again."

Maeve's eyes swam with tears. "What are you saying?" she asked.

"Your mother and I have talked about this," her father continued, "and we're in full agreement. For the next two weeks, no going out after school—or on the weekends. Just school, lessons, and home."

Tears spilled down Maeve's cheeks. But her father wasn't done.

"Maeve, this has been a hard time for all of us. But that doesn't mean that any of us should let up on what we care most about. Our trust for each other, our respect for each other, the consideration that we show each other as a family. You really let us down tonight—and you let your friends down, too."

Maeve struggled to regain her composure. She felt so awful about what had happened. It was horrible being punished. But worst of all was the look of utter disappointment in her parents' eyes.

Her mother put her hand on her father's arm. "Ross, I'm going home. You've got everything under control now." She turned back to Maeve with a sigh. "I'll see you again on Sunday afternoon, Maeve. We can talk more then." She gave her daughter a hug and turned to leave.

Maeve sank down onto the couch, trying to piece together everything that had happened. Suddenly she remembered the dinner party at Avery's the following night.

"Wait," she said, her voice catching. "I'm supposed to go to Avery's house tomorrow night. Remember? Her mom's having that dinner party to raise money for her old school. She asked us all to come over and help her."

Her mother glanced briefly at her father. "Ross?" she asked.

It was strange, Maeve thought. She couldn't remember the last time her parents had seemed to be in such close agreement. It was like they'd scripted all of this!

"What do you think, Carol?" Ross asked, his eyes on hers.

Maeve's mother shrugged. "It's a previous commitment. A responsibility to someone else. I'm okay with it, Maeve, as long as you're back home by nine o'clock. But no activities outside the house tomorrow."

Maeve's father nodded. "I'm fine with that as well. And

tomorrow during the day, Maeve, you can help me unpack."

Maeve nodded dumbly. She didn't really want to think much about tomorrow. It was horrible having her parents so mad at her. But they were her parents. They had to forgive her—one day. What about her friends? How was she ever going to be able to explain to them what had happened? Why she'd lied ... to everyone.

❤··

Notes to Self:
1. Consider moving to an island near Fiji. Maybe people there won't be mad at me.
2. Mom and Dad HAVE to forgive me eventually, don't they? Isn't there a law somewhere about that?
3. Maybe I can offer to let Avery keep Ben and Jen another week???
4. Maybe I can offer to (gulp) help Katani with all that laundry?
5. Maybe I can just tell them all I am so, so, so sorry.
6. Boy, did I learn my lesson.

ᘓ

"You sure you won't go to bed?" her father asked her. It was almost twelve thirty, but Maeve didn't feel ready for bed yet. And it wasn't just the prospect of that bunk bed, either.

"I'll go soon. See you in the morning, Dad," Maeve said.

She started flipping absently through one of the scrapbooks that her father had left on the coffee table. He was still unpacking, and this was one that Maeve hadn't seen before. It looked old.

The front half of the book was filled with faded black-and-white photographs. Her father was a little boy in most of them. Maeve had seen some of these before, and she recognized them right away. Her father at the zoo with her grandfather. Her father sitting in front of a birthday cake shaped like a train. It made her feel a little funny, turning the pages and watching her father's boyhood unfold before her. There was so much the little boy in these pictures didn't know yet. He didn't know that he would fall in love one day with Maeve's mom. That they would have children together, that one day they would decide to separate.

Maeve dashed away a tear. She was beginning to recognize something. Her parents' decision to separate really mattered to her. A lot. That didn't mean she was going to be able to change it or make it better. Trying to be a "model daughter" wasn't the answer either. But neither was thinking that she could make up her own rules and turn her back on her values. She needed to—how had Avery put it?—"take care of herself."

Maeve kept turning the pages. At the back of the album she found a packet of yellowing letters tied with a black ribbon.

Love letters! Maeve thought. Maybe her father had written love letters to her mom ... But even as she thought this, her eye fell on the signature at the bottom of the first letter. *Ma.* In pale, spidery script, slanted and elegant. They were from Nana to Daddy.

Her father had glued one letter carefully into the back of the album. It was a short letter, beautifully penned. Maeve read it slowly.

My dearest Ross,

You asked me today how to stop being a child. How to become a man. Those words touched me so much because I remember asking my own mother. How does one move from childhood to adulthood? I decided to write to you because letters can come from the heart in a way that spoken words sometimes can't.

I can tell you this, my darling boy. Be true to who you are. Be honest. Be fair. Love your friends and your family and treat them with care and respect. The world is full of complexity and challenges, but you'll be equal to them if you remember who you are. At the end of the day, look within your heart and ask yourself this: have I changed the world at all today for the better? If you can say yes, then you are on your way not just to becoming a man, but to becoming a fine human being. I love you, Ross.

Always,

Ma

Maeve traced the letters with her fingers, mouthing the words as she read. She could almost feel her grandmother writing these words to her, through her father, as if her grandmother had reached across the generations to hold her hand and offer her guidance. Maeve didn't feel quite so worried about her friends anymore. She would find a way to explain to them, just as her father had suggested. More important, she had learned a lesson—one that she wouldn't forget. And how had her father put it? Sometimes you need to make mistakes in order to figure out what to do in the future. Anyway, now the future was up to her.

Dear Mom and Dad,

I am writing this letter straight from my heart to tell you how really, truly, totally sorry I am about everything that happened. I know that things are really hard for our family now. And I don't want to be a problem. So, I want you to know that I learned my lesson. And even though you two are living apart now, I know you both love me and always need to know where I am. You don't have to worry about me. I have the best friends in the world and I have the best parents. I think I am a very lucky girl that way. Okay ... I have a good brother, too. I will make you all proud of me.

Your daughter,

Maeve Kaplan-Taylor

P.S. Hugs and Kisses
P.P.S. I knew that if I wrote a letter you would know that I really mean everything I am saying.

CHAPTER
19

Hunting the Elusive Guinea Pig

Avery's Blog

How to Catch a Guinea Pig
1. Set delicious pieces of food around
   the perimeter of your living room.
   Lettuce is good.
2. Try ringing a little bell while
   crawling around on all fours. You may
   look silly, but the guinea pig will
   probably hear you.
3. Bring over another guinea pig as a
   decoy. Have it run around and see if
   it goes someplace, like under the
   curtains, looking for its friend.

Chat Room: BSG

File Edit People View Help

flikchic: did u guys get my apology cards?
skywriter: that's so cool you can send those on e-mail!
flikchic: I really am so sorry guys
lafrida: I think we're all ok—but Katani
4kicks: yeah she's still kind of mad
skywriter: maybe u can talk to her tonight at avery's
flikchic: I wonder if she got the e-card I sent
4kicks: she won't stay mad 4ever.
flikchic: I hope not, I've really learned my lesson
skywriter: was Dillon mad you had to leave?
flikchic: He wasn't but his dad sure was. he missed the last few seconds of the game
4kicks: guess you don't want to know that they won in overtime by 2 points
flikchic: oh well, we saw the whole first part anyway.
4kicks: arggghhh!! g2g, remember, my mom wants help with this party tonight. come over asap if u can!

4 people here

flikchic
skywriter
lafrida
4kicks

Saturday afternoon, two catering trucks were parked in front of Avery's house when she got back from soccer practice. A woman was setting up folding chairs in the dining room and another was deep in discussion with Avery's mother in the kitchen.

Her mother called "hello" to Avery but was clearly distracted. "You'll have to forgive me, honey," she said. "We're in the final stages of planning for tonight. Go ahead and make yourself a snack. We should be done in about half an hour."

Avery dumped her soccer bag in the front hall and began to race upstairs. She had to clean the guinea pig cage and she had to find Beckham. This was getting serious. Suddenly, she turned around and headed downstairs to the kitchen where Carla was working on the famous Caesar salad, the only thing she had to make for tonight since the caterers were doing the rest. Carla didn't usually help out on Saturday, but she'd come in today to help Avery's mom.

Avery got some newspapers from the recycling bin. And some large scissors to shred them with from the kitchen drawer. Carla was looking at her strangely. Avery knew that taking trash back into the house just before a party was not something Carla approved of.

"I have to clean their cages," Avery said to Carla.

"The little rodent cages?" Carla clearly did not approve of Avery's adopted pets.

"They're guinea pigs," Avery said, offended. "And their names are Hamm and Beckham."

"Ham … back-ham … pigs should be bacon, not pets," Carla said.

When Avery reached her room, it was in better shape than she thought it would be. Carla had done her usual magic. She had cleaned everything—except the cage. Avery was relieved to see it sitting in the corner, untouched, and rodent or bacon, Carla had left Hamm alone.

Was it possible, or did Hamm actually seem excited to see her? As Avery approached the cage, Hamm sniffed the bars and rolled on her back. It made her laugh. Hamm had real talent. She was going to have to remember to talk to Maeve about letting her continue to coach her. And Beckham, She was great. She could be a stunt guinea pig in some movie or something! If she could just find her. She wasn't completely panicked yet because she had seen an article on the Internet about a guinea pig that was found after being lost for three months in the backyard.

Avery was still thinking about the article as she cleaned the cage, laying down the new shredded newspaper—sports pages and entertainment sections only. She checked her watch as she went. Only a half hour until people started to get here. Maybe she could still find Beckham.

Avery swallowed hard. But what if she couldn't? How was she going to tell Maeve she'd lost one of her guinea pigs? Her poor friend was already traumatized, as her weird behavior the night before plainly demonstrated. And on top of all of that, now she was going to have to find out Beckham was gone!

Avery decided another search was in order. She looked everywhere—even in the basement. But there was still no sign of a guinea pig. Nothing.

She bumped into Carla, on her way up from the laundry room with table linens.

"Uh, Carla?" asked Avery. "You haven't seen any little creatures running around down here, have you?"

Carla stared at her. "Little creatures?" she repeated. "If

you mean that little guinea pig of yours, yes, I saw her, but not down here."

Avery jumped up and down, throwing her arms around Carla. Beckham was saved!

Carla tried to keep the laundry from toppling over. "She's right in your closet. I didn't think you wanted your mother to find out," she added. "So I kept the door closed. Did I do the right thing?"

"Carla, you are my savior." Avery gave her another hug and ran right upstairs.

Avery ran upstairs two at a time and burst into her room. Disaster. Her closet door was open. Darn! She forgot she had opened it to put her gear away. And to top it all off she had left her bedroom door open. Beckham could be anywhere by now. Maybe she just wasn't meant to have pets. First the Marty fiasco and now this. The girls were going to be here any minute. She was going to have to tell Maeve the truth, and ask her friends for help. At least Beckham was in the house. She hoped.

SAVED BY THE BELL

Isabel, Charlotte, and Maeve were waiting for Avery at the door.

Avery's mother had called all the parents with a personal invitation for their daughter to come to the event. Maeve's father felt it would be rude for Maeve not to attend. Maeve's mind wasn't on guinea pigs though. "Where is Katani? Is she still mad at me?" Maeve asked nervously. "I am so sorry about all of this. Really, I am. I just don't know how to make everything right."

Avery cleared her throat. Maybe this wasn't the best moment to further destroy Maeve's life by telling her about Beckham. On the other hand ... well, Maeve was going to find out for herself in about five minutes, when she looked in the guinea pigs' cage upstairs and noticed there was exactly ONE little guy in there. Not two. Avery took a deep breath.

"Speaking of things not being right," she said, trying for the right tone. Somehow it didn't come out very well though. She sounded a little too flippant. "Uh ... Maeve," she said, when everyone turned to stare at her. "I have good news ... and bad news."

"I could use some good news," Maeve said, looking at her. "I'm not sure I'm all that psyched for more bad news."

"Well," Avery said quickly, "here's the good news. Hamm is doing just great. And she really seems to like having a bit more extra room in her cage."

"Hamm?" Maeve repeated blankly, staring at her.

"Uh ... yeah. Ben. Or Jen, I'm not sure which one it is. But I renamed them, see, after Mia Hamm and David Beckham. My two favorite soccer stars."

"That's so cute," said Charlotte.

"Hamm," Maeve repeated slowly. She was still staring at Avery. "Hamm ... likes having more space? That's the good news?" She looked horrified. "Avery, what's the bad news? What happened to the other one? Beckett?"

"BECKHAM," Avery corrected her. "You know, *Bend It Like Beckham*?"

Maeve was starting to turn red again. "What happened to him? I mean her? Avery, I trusted you! My guineas are like my ... my ... babies," she sputtered.

"Calm down," Avery whispered. The caterers were turning around to stare at them. "I'm sure she's perfectly fine. It's just ... well ... I don't know exactly where she is, that's all."

"You LOST my guinea pig?" Maeve shrieked. "Avery, how could you?"

"I swear, all I did was turn around for one tiny second. I had them both out of their cage so they could run around a little. You told me they NEED exercise," Avery defended herself. "And my mom came in to talk to me, and she must've sneaked out while we were talking. The door was barely open a CRACK. Then Carla found her and put her in the closet, but I didn't know that ... I left the closet door open ... I'm sorry."

Maeve calmed down enough to think for a minute. "That sounds like Ben," she admitted. "I told you—she's an escape artist. But you should've been watching!" she scolded.

"Look, I'm sorry," Avery cried. "It's not like ANY of us is perfect," she added defensively, shooting Maeve a look.

Maeve didn't say anything. She just stood silent.

"That's not fair, Avery," Isabel added sharply.

"You're right. I've just been so worried," stammered Avery. "Maeve, I've looked everywhere. But I can't seem to find her! My mom's been so focused on this dinner party tonight ... there's all these caterers setting up for it ... I'm scared someone's going to leave the door open ... and she'll escape."

This was a terrible thought to contemplate. What a really bad weekend.

"Maeve," she said miserably, hanging her head, "I've totally failed you. I swear, once we find Beckham, I'm not going to beg my mom for a pet anymore. And I'll figure out some way to make this up to you ... and Beckham. I promise!"

When Maeve saw how miserable Avery looked, she couldn't stay mad at her. She knew what it was like to make a big mistake. "Let's just find her, Avery," Maeve said. She assured her, "she's done the same thing with me. I had a friend who lost a guinea pig once for three weeks. It was so fat that it got stuck behind a piece of furniture and couldn't get out until it lost weight. Then it squeezed out. Let's just see if we can find her. Okay?"

"She's probably under the eaves somewhere," Maeve said. "Or in a closet or under a bureau," Maeve suggested. "She likes small spaces."

"Don't worry," Charlotte said to them both. "We'll find her as soon as the party is over."

Avery looked at herself in the mirror with a groan. "WHY?" she wailed. "Why would anyone possibly think that dressing like this is a good idea?"

That broke the tension for the moment.

Maeve and Isabel exchanged amused glances. Avery managed to make her navy skirt and white sweater look like a suit of armor. She stood stiffly, arms out at her sides, a pinched and miserable look on her face. The way she walked suggested that her feet—in flats—were already killing her, and they hadn't even left her bedroom yet.

They could hear the caterers busily setting up for dinner downstairs. Avery's mother was rushing around like crazy, trying to finish getting dressed while calling out last-minute instructions about what needed to go where. Apparently Mr. Jameson, the big benefactor whom they were trying so hard to impress, was supposed to be seated at the head of the table, with Avery's mother right at his side. The girls were way down at the other end with Scott.

"Avery! Have you seen the dining room? It looks like a really fancy restaurant in there!" Maeve exclaimed. Unlike Avery, Maeve loved fancy parties and getting dressed up. If it weren't for her worries about Katani and Beckham, this would be Maeve's idea of a perfect evening.

Speaking of Katani, she was walking toward them. "Hi. I'm sorry I'm late. My mother had to drop off a brief to a client. What's up?" She looked at everyone but Maeve. Maeve had the impression that Katani was trying to pretend she wasn't there. She wouldn't even catch Maeve's eye.

Distracting herself, Maeve picked up a piece of paper from Avery's desk. "What's this?"

"Oh ..." Avery said mournfully, picking it up and studying it. "It's some information I downloaded from Google on guinea pigs. Did you know that they're descendants of South American rodents, and that they have three distinct sounds—a whistle, a purr, and a squeal?"

Maeve looked sad. "Poor Ben," she said.

"What happened to Ben?" asked Katani with sudden concern.

"She escaped," said Maeve mournfully.

"We can't find her anywhere," explained Isabel.

All five girls shared a moment of silence, thinking about the missing guinea pig.

"Jen is really missing her," Maeve added. When she saw Avery's face she added, "I didn't mean to make you feel bad! Don't worry, Avery. You did everything you possibly could!"

"Anyway," Katani snapped, "who should be making WHO feel bad around here?" She crossed her arms indignantly.

The other girls looked at each other and rolled their eyes.

"She could still turn up," Isabel insisted. "You guys shouldn't lose hope."

There was no time left to worry about Ben/Beckham. The doorbell was ringing—and it looked like the first guests had arrived.

Avery's mother knocked on the door. "You girls look lovely," she said, smiling at all of them with the slightly distracted look she always got on her face when she was in "entertainment" mode. "Now, did Avery explain to you that Mr. Jameson is a VERY IMPORTANT businessman? We're hoping that he's going to give Talbot Academy a large donation. His daughters went there quite a while ago. He may want to ask you girls what it's like being twelve or thirteen these days."

"He's not going to try to ship us off to the Talbot Academy, is he?" Avery asked uneasily.

"Of course not!" Avery's mother said. From the look she gave Avery, it was clear that the thought had crossed her mind once or twice. "Come on, girls. Time to meet and mingle. Don't look so scared; everyone is dying to meet you all."

The five girls trooped obediently down the winding staircase to the Maddens' enormous living room. Katani was still acting distant toward Maeve. Avery had stepped on the backs of her shoes so they were only half on, and she was helping herself to nuts from a small bowl on a coffee table. Charlotte and Isabel were standing around feeling awkward and self-conscious, wondering what they were going to say to all the guests who seemed to be peering at them like they were specimens in a laboratory.

"Sorry, people, I know this is kind of boring," Avery said.

Suddenly Maeve grabbed her arm. Her face had a funny look on it.

"Avery—did you hear that?"

Avery stared at her. "The doorbell?"

"No! I think I heard a whistle! A guinea pig whistle!"

"Omigod!" Avery shouted.

Her mother happened to be coming into the living room, her hand through the arm of a distinguished looking elderly gentleman. She gave Avery an encouraging look before turning back to the gentleman. "Lewis, this is my daughter, Avery, and several of her school friends," she said in an upbeat voice. "Katani, Charlotte, Maeve, and Isabel, say hello to Mr. Jameson." Mr. Jameson extended his hand to each girl and by name told them how glad he was to meet them.

Avery was looking furtively around the room. Was it possible that Beckham was really here somewhere? She wished her mother would go and introduce Mr. Jameson to the other guests so she could get down on all fours and look for him!

"Avery," her mother said, "Mr. Jameson is asking you a question."

Avery sighed. Okay, the search for Beckham was going to have to wait. She wriggled around to try to make her skirt less bunchy and let her mother drag her through a bunch of tedious questions about being twelve and a half. "Well, Mr. Jameson. I guess it's kind of like it always was—you know, school, friends, sports. The biggest difference is that we have I.M."

Mr. Jameson smiled. "Yes, I know about I.M. I use it with my grandkids. It's a great way to stay connected."

Avery gave him an admiring look. *Not bad for an old guy*, she thought. But she wondered if Mr. Jameson would be surprised to know that the only thing this twelve-and-a-half-year-old was really thinking about was a missing guinea pig!

❦

"I heard her. I swear, I heard her," Maeve insisted as they walked away. It was five minutes to six, and any minute the girls were going to follow the grown-ups into the splendidly decorated dining room.

"Are you sure?" Katani demanded.

One good thing: worrying about Beckham was making Katani forget about being mad. She seemed to be thawing a little bit. And getting into the spirit of the hunt.

There were almost fifty people packed into the Maddens' living room, and now that it was crowded enough, the girls were using every free second to try to hunt for Beckham. Even Maeve was calling her Beckham now! She was almost certain she caught a glimpse of her running along the floorboard in the living room, but if it really was her, she was moving awfully fast.

"It could've just been a shadow," she admitted regretfully. "It's a little dim in here—it's kind of hard to see."

"I know. My mom calls it mood lighting," Avery said.

"Girls," Mrs. Madden announced, putting a hand on Avery's shoulder and Maeve's, and steering them toward the dining room, "It's time for dinner now. Please take your places."

Maeve and Avery looked at each other helplessly. There was no choice but to follow her orders and head to the dining room. The hunt for Beckham was going to have to wait until dinner was over.

ભ

Avery's mother decided that toasts and speeches should come right at the beginning of the meal.

"I'm starving," Avery groaned to Maeve and Isabel, who were sitting on either side of her at the end of the table farthest from their honored guest.

Charlotte couldn't believe how fancy everything was. Two crystal glasses at each place, and tons of silverware. The catering staff had dressed up in black and white uniforms and they were running around filling up water and wine glasses like real waiters. It was kind of intimidating, not to mention majorly cool! How did they get a table big enough to seat all these people? Avery explained that they added on to the regular table with rented ones, but still! It looked like something right out of a fancy magazine.

Mrs. Madden got up to make a speech about her years at Talbot Academy. Charlotte found herself tuning out a little. She caught parts of it—stuff about "values" and "traditions" and "impressionable girls" and "making a fine contribution to society." But mostly, she was watching the other people at the table. They were all looking eagerly at Mr. Jameson. He must be really important, Charlotte thought, if so many people cared so much about impressing him.

While Mrs. Madden was speaking, the caterers brought in the salad bowl. Charlotte had never seen anything remotely like it. It was ten times as big as the biggest salad bowl she and her dad had at home. And because it was silver—or at least, it LOOKED like silver—it was incredibly impressive, like something you'd see in a medieval castle.

It took two of the caterers to lift the bowl onto the table. Apparently, everyone was supposed to look longingly at the salad while Mrs. Madden talked, and then while Mr. Jameson talked, and then, FINALLY, they would serve the salad to everyone.

Charlotte wriggled in her seat. She was getting a little restless. This was all so formal.

Oh good. Mrs. Madden was sinking back into her seat, beaming, while everyone clapped politely. Now it was Mr. Jameson's turn. He got to his feet, lifting his glass, and began to cough.

"AVERY," Maeve whispered frantically, tugging at her friend's sleeve.

"Maeve, we have to be quiet," ordered Avery.

"No ... you have to look." Avery turned to follow Maeve's gaze. She was staring, stricken, at the enormous salad bowl. Charlotte followed her gaze, as did Katani and Isabel. Five pairs of eyes widened.

There, in the middle of the enormous bowl of salad, was Beckham, lifting her little head curiously right out of the middle of the bowl and sniffing wildly around her. She had bits of leaves in her mouth to show that she'd already tasted the lettuce, and it looked like she thought it was pretty good.

"And THAT," Mr. Jameson said, setting down his wine glass, "is why it is vitally important to incorporate some of these programs into the curriculum." Everyone gave a short round of applause, guessing from the sound of his voice that his speech was only just getting started.

Everyone, that is, but the five Beacon Street Girls. They were watching in fascinated horror as Beckham wriggled her way free of the lettuce, crawled to the edge of the salad bowl, and looking down like a diver from the high dive at an enormous swimming pool, jumped deftly onto the white linen tablecloth and scampered right down the center of the table toward Maeve and Avery.

"BECKHAM!" Avery shrieked, jumping up to make a lunge for the guinea pig.

"AVERY!" her mother cried, horrified.

Total mayhem broke out.

The women who were sitting on either side of the salad bowl jumped up, knocking over their wineglasses. One of them knocked over a chair in her hurry. Several other guests actually screamed, which Avery thought was a little much, but it must have been the shock, as she told Maeve later.

Nobody could scream at the sight of Beckham otherwise. A few guests began to laugh hysterically.

The guests were on their feet in an instant, pushing their chairs back and knocking into each other as they tried to get away from what Charlotte heard one woman call "that ENORMOUS RAT!"

"It's not a rat," Carla corrected her from the butler's pantry. "It's a pig."

"It's a guinea pig." Avery corrected them again. "It's not a rodent. It's a pet."

"Avery, I thought you had that thing in a CAGE," her mother frantically shouted, looking around her at the upset table with an expression of mingled embarrassment, anger, and—was it possible?—just the slightest touch of humor, too.

"Beckham's an escape artist," Avery said, chasing after the little rodent, with Maeve in hot pursuit right after her.

They made quite a sight, as Charlotte informed them later. And really, if it hadn't been for Mr. Jameson and all the trouble that Avery's mom had gone to making the dinner so fancy, everyone had to admit that they really looked hilarious. Five girls chasing one very fast guinea pig. And much to their amazement, Mr. Jameson, in his fancy suit, decided to help with the chase!

☙

"Well," Katani said philosophically, when the mess had been straightened up and Beckham had been safely cornered, "I guess Mr. Jameson got a little more of today's girls' extracurricular activities than he bargained for."

Avery kept showering Beckham with kisses, her brown eyes rapturous. "Who knew," she said with admiration. "I thought he was just a boring old guy. But it turns out he used to have a pair of guinea pigs named Milton and Plato." Her mother had been impressed by what she kept referring to (over and over again) as Mr. Jameson's "understanding." But Avery was just as impressed that a man his age could catch a guinea pig. Especially one stuck behind the radiator. Mr. Jameson calmly walked back to the table, got a piece of lettuce, wiped the dressing off, and then sat on the floor and held the lettuce until Beckham came to him.

"It was totally cool," said Avery.

Everyone watched in admiring silence as Beckham perched on his hand and munched on the lettuce. "I rest my case," he said to the admiring crowd, who almost broke into applause, then stopped clapping, not wanting to disturb Beckham and send her running off to parts unknown again.

"That," Avery said with evident satisfaction, "was the most fun dinner party I've ever been to in this house! Beckham was a real superstar and she really broke the ice. Everyone had so much fun afterwards."

The Beacon Street Girls started laughing. "It was pretty impressive, I'll say that much," Katani admitted. She glanced at Maeve with a shy grin. Somehow, chasing Beckham around had helped her to feel a little more forgiving toward Maeve.

"So you're not really mad at me anymore?" Maeve whispered to her.

Katani shook her head. "You know me, Maeve. I huff and I puff, but I don't stay mad forever." She gave Maeve a quick hug. "But promise you won't do that to us ever again," she insisted. "I was scared for you."

Maeve's eyes lit up. "I promise. And even better, know what I'm going to do to make it up to you?"

Her friends looked at her a little apprehensively.

"Maybe we should just let it go," Charlotte began.

But there was no stopping Maeve. "Charlotte, can I borrow the Tower? I want to throw a sleepover party there in two weeks—for all five of us. I want to make it up to you guys for being ... well, the way I've been lately."

"Okay," Charlotte said with a smile. "I'll check with my dad, but it sounds good to me!"

Maeve scooped Beckham up for one last snuggle. "I could bring Beckham ..." she began.

But four voices cried out "NO" in unison.

Beckham, it appeared, was ready to go back to Maeve's house with Hamm. And it looked like she'd had all the salad she could eat for the foreseeable future.

CR

Sunday afternoon, Maeve was sitting in front of her laptop at her dad's kitchen table, wondering if a pink font would be inspirational. She was trying to think of the best way to tell Dillon how bad she felt about Friday night. She typed out a few sample e-mails.

"I had so much fun on Friday night. Sorry about the last quarter, but—"

No. Too light-hearted.

"I am SO SO SORRY." Maeve liked this one—the double "so" was her latest touch, and she thought it added a nice, personal emphasis. "Please tell your dad that, too. It was kind of a family emergency. Yours, Maeve."

She liked that one. She opened up her e-mail and sent it off with a little ping.

Hopefully, Dillon would understand. She wasn't so sure about his father.

Just then, the door to her dad's apartment opened and Sam came in. He was walking slowly and he looked like he'd hurt his hand.

"Where've you been?" Maeve asked.

"In the park," he muttered. He was trying not to look at her in that funny way boys do when they think that YOU won't see THEM.

"Hey," she said, taking a closer look at him. "Are you Okay? You don't look right."

Sam stared at her, his lip wobbling. "I got in a fight," he muttered.

Maeve stared at him. Her brother Sam—in a FIGHT? For a kid who played war games 24-7, Sam loathed any kind of physical violence. He didn't even like playing football because it was too rough.

"It was Joey. He is SUCH a creep. He told me Mom and Dad aren't EVER going to get back together again." Sam sniffled. "He told me that they're probably going to get DIVORCED. He said that's what always happens when parents say they need to separate for a little while."

Maeve suddenly felt a wave of pity wash over her. Her brother looked so small and vulnerable. She jumped up and put her arms around him, engulfing him with warmth.

"What a mean thing to say. He doesn't even KNOW Mom and Dad," she told him.

Sam stared up at her, his brown eyes questioning. "Maeve? Do you think Mom and Dad are ever going to get back together?"

Hearing her brother ask that question made Maeve stop short.

Maeve looked at his face, and swallowed hard. Part of her wanted nothing more than to wrap her arms around him and assure him that they WOULD. But the look on his face made her hesitate.

"I don't know," she said softly. "But Sam—"

He waited, and she cleared her throat.

"I know things are going to be okay for all of us," she said finally.

"Okay," he said. Just that—okay. But he actually looked a little bit less miserable. And he trotted off to their room, looking for his *Giant Book of War Facts*.

Go figure, Maeve thought. That seemed to be enough for him.

Maybe what she'd said to Sam wasn't actually that far from the truth. Maybe everything WAS going to be okay. That might not mean knowing what was going to happen. At this point, Maeve wasn't so sure that her parents would get back together. But she had the sense that they were going to pull through as a family, no matter what.

CHAPTER

20

The Heritage Museum

O kay," Ms. O'Reilly said with a smile. "Who feels like going first? Ms. Rodriguez tells me you've done a fantastic job with your written reports, and she's joining us today to hear your presentations."

It was Monday, and fourth-period social studies was devoted to the Heritage Museum project. Each day this week, kids would be taking turns reading their reports out loud and sharing some of the things they'd brought in from home.

"Remember," Ms. O'Reilly added, "each of you has imagined this project a little differently, and that's part of the point. Our hope isn't to have twenty-one identical projects. Some of you have been researching topics related to your own family's history. Some of you have very personal objects to share, some have found cultural or historical artifacts." She looked intently around the room. "Any takers for going first?"

Katani raised her hand. "I'll go first," she volunteered.

Ms. O'Reilly was delighted. "Katani, why don't you come to the front of the room, and share what you have so far with the rest of us?"

Katani nodded. She walked gracefully up to the front of the room, leaning back against Ms. O'Reilly's desk and holding up a black-and-white photograph of what looked like a small church.

"Does anyone recognize this building?" she asked.

Nobody did.

Katani smiled. "Well, I didn't know it either, before I started working on this report. It's actually called the African Meeting House, and it's the oldest black church in Boston. It's on Beacon Hill, on a street called Smith Court, and you can still visit it today."

Katani cleared her throat. "So, you're probably wondering what this Meeting House has to do with me. Well, I started doing my research by talking to my grandmother, Principal Fields." She grinned. "I think you all know who she is ..."

A few people laughed. Others just nodded.

"Well, she started to tell me a little bit about the history of education for African Americans here in Boston, and I decided that I wanted to learn more. So I guess my research is more ... what Ms. Rodriguez said, more general, rather than being superpersonal." Katani held up the picture again. "This church became a very important meeting place for African Americans in Boston in the nineteenth century. Lots of famous activists met there—including Frederick Douglass, Harriet Tubman, and Sojourner Truth. It started to be called 'The Abolitionist Church' because so many people who came there were fighting slavery." Katani cleared her throat. "But the most interesting thing to me is that in 1835, a school was opened right next to this Meeting House, which was called the Abiel Smith School. It was one of the first black schools in Boston. So I guess I chose to bring in this photograph for two reasons. First, because I didn't know this building was right here in Boston and how important it was for African Americans. And second, because the building became a symbol for the courage and determination of people who wanted education for themselves and their children."

"Well done, Katani!" both Ms. O'Reilly and Ms. Rodriguez exclaimed.

Katani looked really proud.

"If I may interject, I like the way you wove your own personal history into something much wider," Ms. Rodriguez added.

Charlotte offered to go next. She had brought in several objects to share: her vintage denim jacket, a brass pocket telescope, and a camera.

"The first object that I want to show is this old camera. It belonged to my great-grandfather Jonathan Ramsey. He moved to Massachusetts from Virginia with his family in the 1940s to be a newspaper photographer. Before that he was part of team of photographers who worked for the United States Farm Securities Administration during the Great Depression in the 1930s. Their assignment was to 'introduce Americans to America.' Remember, at that time, we didn't have televisions yet, and some people didn't even have radio. My great-grandfather's job was to show how the Depression was affecting the lives of the Blue Ridge mountain people of Virginia."

"This is one of his pictures." Charlotte held up a black-and-white photo of a mountain family sitting on the porch of a dilapidated shack. The mother and the father looked really tired but the four children were smiling shyly. "My great-grandfather wrote a note on the back of this picture," Charlotte added. "Hard-working, proud people. Their lives are difficult but they do not complain."

Ms. O'Reilly walked to the front of the class and asked Charlotte if she could see the photograph. "People," she said. "This is an important piece of documentary photography. Photographs like these highlighted the suffering and the joys of small-town and rural America during the Great Depression—the worst economic crisis this country has ever faced.

"Wonderful research, Charlotte. I am thrilled that you could share this with us," she said to Charlotte.

Charlotte beamed. The next object that she held up was the denim jacket. "This was my mom's," she said. Her voice caught a little, but she went on. "My mom died when I was four. She was a teacher and she loved to read poetry and dance to old-time rock and roll music. She loved this jacket and now it's my good-luck charm. I don't know if this jacket is really history, but I wear it whenever I feel like I need special inspiration."

Everyone was quiet for a moment before Charlotte went on.

"And this," she said, holding up the folding telescope, "belonged to my mother's father. Before I started talking to my dad, I didn't know that my grandfather loved astronomy too. He actually worked as a pharmacist, but he was really passionate about studying the stars. He always said that if he saved up enough money he wanted to go back to school. So I brought these three things in to show different things that have been really important in my family. What I learned is that some of the things I love most, my family did, too, and that they really connect me back to my parents and grandparents."

"Nice work, Charlotte," Ms. O'Reilly said approvingly. She turned to the class. "I especially like how very differently Katani and Charlotte handled this assignment. But you can see how much thought and care both put into choosing what they wanted to study."

One by one, other students shared artifacts and stories about their families. Isabel brought in a beautiful silver comb studded with turquoise that had belonged to her great-aunt. "My sister is starting to plan her Quinceañera," she told the class. "That's a very special tradition in my heritage. It honors a girl when she turns fifteen. Elena Maria is going to wear this hair comb on that day. And two years from now, when it's my turn for my Quinceañera, I'll wear it too."

Riley brought in some sheet music from a song that his father had written when he was in college. Samantha Simmons brought in a strand of pearls that had been handed down from one generation to the next in her family. She couldn't leave them because they were so precious, but she wanted everyone to see them. Before long, the Heritage Museum began to grow and grow. There were college pennants, suitcases, maps, photographs, and even a baseball bat, which Dillon brought in because he had a second cousin who played in the minor leagues.

Avery raised her hand. "I brought in three things from three different families," she said.

Anna rolled her eyes. "This is all supposed to be about YOUR family," she said. "Didn't you follow instructions?"

Avery gave her a look. "I did. It's just that I actually HAVE three families. My dad's family, my mom's, and my birth parents' family." Ms. Rodriguez glared at Anna to be quiet. Anna shrugged her shoulders and turned around.

"Avery, come up and show us what you've brought in," Ms. O'Reilly said encouragingly.

"I'll start with my dad. He's a mountain guy," Avery said with a grin. "Loves mountains: biking, snowboarding, skiing.

You name it. He lives in Colorado and he's the one who taught me how to snowboard. So I brought in a picture of where he lives. It's called Telluride, and it's totally awesome. But it turns out that my dad's dad also loved mountains. He used to climb them, not slide down them—but I think it's all part of the same thing." Avery shrugged. "The second thing I brought in is from my birth parents. It's called a *bojagi*. It's a special cloth used to carry things in Korea, and I found it when I was looking through some old stuff in the loft of my mom's carriage house. It's special to me because it came from them. But when I did research on it, it turns out that it's an important symbol. Some people say that it's a metaphor in Korean writing for something that holds a lot of stuff together in one place. Even though the pieces are different, it can still hold a lot. Like a family."

Everyone was quiet again, even Anna. Avery cleared her throat. "The last thing that I brought in is to remind me of my mom."

Avery took out a bottle of water and held it up.

Anna snickered, giving Joline one of her famous scornful looks.

"Anna," Ms. O'Reilly said warningly. "Avery, can you tell us a little bit more about why you chose this?"

Avery nodded. "I found a quote," she told the class, "that's about adoption. I really liked it, and it helped me to understand something amazing about my mom that I never really knew before." She took out a piece of paper. "Here it goes: 'A mother is like a mountain spring that nourishes the tree at the root. But one who mothers another's child is like a water that rises into a cloud and goes a long distance to nourish a lone tree in the desert.'"

"It's from something called *The Talmud*." She shrugged,

folding the piece of paper again. "So that's why I brought in this bottle of water. My mom—she's like the water in here. She went a long way to find me. And I guess I'm kind of like that tree."

Everyone was quiet for a moment. Then Maeve began to clap—quietly at first, and then louder and louder. Soon the whole class was clapping, even Anna and Joline. Avery shrugged, smiled, and sat down again.

"Maeve, how about you?" Ms. O'Reilly asked.

Maeve got slowly to her feet. "I'm still working on mine," she said.

Anna snickered meanly and Maeve felt her face redden.

"Anna. I'm going to have to ask you to be considerate of your classmates, or step out into the hall until you CAN be," Ms. O'Reilly said firmly.

Maeve took a deep breath. "I'm learning a lot of things about my family that I didn't know," she said, ignoring Anna. "But I wanted to start with something I found that was written by my father's mother." She held up one of her grandmother's letters for the class to see.

"For me, this assignment started one way and ended up another way." Maeve cleared her throat. "To be honest, at first I thought it was just kind of ... you know, boring." A few people in the room chuckled. "But the more I thought about it, the more I found out that there was stuff I really wanted to know about ... from people in my family who I'd never met ... or who died before I was born. I found these letters that my grandmother wrote to my father before he started college. He saved them because they're all about life. How to be a good person. How to listen to yourself. My dad calls them 'letters from the heart' because he says that's the way my grandmother was when she wrote them. It was like she was just pouring herself out to him. So I brought this one in, and I wanted to include it because I think ..." Maeve tried to find the perfect words. "Letters like this are like personal diaries. They tell us what kind of values people had, how they used words to express themselves, and what was important to them. I also have a playbill from the 1930s from a show called *No, No, Nanette*. My great-grandmother was a Broadway dancer. Back then people liked fun comedies with music and dancing. My grandmother told me that these types of shows helped people take their minds off all their money worries from the Great Depression. I think that if we're lucky, we can learn that kind of stuff from our families. Whoever our families are."

She sat down, realizing then how much it had meant to her to be able to say this in front of the class. A few people turned around to smile at her, and Dillon gave her a big thumbs-up sign. Maeve settled back in her chair with a mixture of pride and relief. And Nana's letter took pride of place along with the other artifacts in the Heritage Museum. A hairclip. A letter. A pocket telescope. An old photograph. And a bottle of water. A stranger coming into the class would have no idea that these things could mean so much to the different people who had brought them in.

But maybe that was the point, Maeve thought. Maybe that was partly an answer to Ms. O'Reilly's question about history. History was what you kept, and the memories those things invoked. The things you carried. And the way that you carried those things—like the bojagi—gave that story its shape.

☙

"It was so cool, Mom. You would've loved what Avery said." Maeve was in the kitchen that night, helping her mother do the dishes and telling her about the class Heritage

Museum. Sam was in his room doing his homework, and it was just the two of them. But it didn't feel lonely or weird tonight. It felt kind of peaceful. Maeve sighed. She hadn't realized what a big deal it was for her to spend her first weekend at her dad's and come back again. She looked around the kitchen. Everything looked the same, but different. It was hard to believe that one day, she could feel as much at home at Dad's place as she did here. But Maeve saw now how that might be possible.

"Mom," Maeve said, drying a plate. "What was it like when you and Daddy first met each other?"

"Wow, that was a long time ago," Maeve's mother said with a smile. "We were both in high school then, can you believe it? I was only fifteen, not that much older than you are now."

She was quiet for a minute, remembering. "Your dad was a few years older than I was. My mother wasn't that crazy about us dating, to tell you the truth. But Daddy and I persevered. We used to have so much fun together! We were really different in lots of ways. Dad was always much less worried than I was about day-to-day stuff like bills. He always had the sense that things would work out in the long run." She smiled. "And you know what? He was usually right!"

"So what happened?" Maeve asked. "Why did you guys stop loving each other?"

Maeve's mother looked at her thoughtfully. "I actually still love your father. And he loves me too. It's just that the way that we love each other has changed. It's more like— well, almost like we're siblings these days. Siblings who don't get along as well as we should," she added ruefully. "This is going to sound like a cliché, but the thing about clichés is that they're often true! We met way too young, and we grew up in different ways. I think together we found ourselves stuck in roles that haven't been the best for us."

"You seem kind of different now," Maeve admitted. "You're not mad the way you used to be. You're not always yelling at Sam and me." She stopped, realizing that what she had just said didn't sound all that nice. "Sorry! I just meant, you seem happier."

Her mom smiled. "Don't worry about hurting my feelings. And you're right, Maeve. The thing is, Daddy and I were in this bad place where he was always expecting me to behave one way, and I was expecting him to behave another. It trapped us both. I think we're both feeling better now. This was a very hard step to take, but it was the right one. For now."

Maeve thought about the question her brother had asked her yesterday. She was dying to ask her mother the same thing. *Would her parents get back together again?*

But she knew it wasn't fair to ask her mom. Not now.

Her mother almost seemed to read her mind. "Maeve," she said softly. "I don't think you have any idea how much we love you. Or how proud you make us—all the time." Her mother cleared her throat. "I know before Dad moved out that I was in a really bad state. I felt so much tension, and I think I took a lot of things out on you. I kept trying to micromanage your schedule, to push you in school, and then the evening with Dillon ... I blame myself a little, Maeve. Dad and I were very distracted. But Maeve, you must promise me to never lie to us when you want to do something."

Maeve couldn't believe it. It was so strange to hear her mother talking to her like this—like they were equals. "I promise, Mom. It all got so out of control. I didn't know what to do," Maeve said.

"That's especially when you should come to me or your

father and tell the truth, honey. I understand better than you think. I'm here to help you," her mother said, as she patted Maeve's hand. "Anyway, since Dad moved out, I've watched all that you've been doing, and it's pretty amazing. I'm not just talking about how much you've pitched in to help out around the house. I've watched how much work you've put into organizing your own schedule, working on your homework, taking real initiative and above all, how much you've helped Sammy." Her mother's eyes glowed. "I'm proud of you, Maeve. Really, really proud. I just want you to know that."

Maeve gulped. "Thanks," she whispered.

They sat together for a while in companionable silence. Finally Maeve dared to ask the question that had been on her mind for weeks. "Do you think you and Daddy are going to get divorced?" she managed to ask.

Her mother sighed. "I don't know. Not now, anyway. We need time to figure things out. But Daddy and I are continuing to meet with a marriage counselor. We both have a lot of talking and listening to do, and we think that would be a good place to start."

Maeve gave her mom a hug. "Thanks for telling me," she said.

Maeve felt ready now to deal with whatever happened. She loved both of her parents with all her heart, and she knew that they loved her too.

And in the end, wasn't that what really mattered?

CHAPTER

21

The Second Awards Ceremony

Pretty good party, Maeve," Katani said, helping herself to more potato chips and dip. She looked around the Tower with appreciation. "I like the streamers and the balloons. It kind of feels like a birthday without the birthday, if you know what I mean."

"Exactly," Maeve said. "That's exactly the way it SHOULD feel."

"Remember when we were chasing Beckham around under Avery's dining room table?" Isabel giggled. "That was hilarious!"

"Hey," Avery said, excited. "I didn't tell you guys what Mr. Jameson said. He called my mom and told her that he had a wonderful time at the dinner party. Mostly thanks to Beckham! He thinks Beckham would make a great mascot for Talbot Academy. He also told her that he liked our 'spirit.' He said—how did he put it—that we represent the strong-willed girls of the early twenty-first century."

"Wow." Everyone was impressed.

"So does that mean your mom isn't mad?" Katani asked.

Avery shook her head. "Nope. She thought it was pretty funny, too. Though she IS making me help pay for some of the broken glasses out of my allowance." Avery flipped her yo-yo. "She even said we could talk about me getting a little furry something. Maybe. IF she isn't allergic to it. Have any of you guys ever heard of a chinchilla? They are the cutest little things—and they're cousins of guinea pigs!"

"Uh-oh," Maeve said. "Watch out, world!"

"So, Maeve," Isabel said, propping herself up on one elbow. "What ever happened with Dillon? Did he forgive you for making him leave the basketball game early?"

Maeve smiled. "Funny you should ask," she said lightly. "He just emailed me today and asked if I wanted to see a movie with him." Her eyes sparkled. "He actually asked if I wanted to see the FIRST HALF of a movie. But I think he was just kidding."

"What'd you say?" Charlotte demanded.

Maeve flipped back her hair. "What do you think?" she demanded. When everyone looked at her expectantly, she filled in the rest. "I told him that I have to ask my parents first and that I'd buy the tickets!" she added with a rueful smile.

Everyone laughed, and Maeve jumped to her feet.

"Okay, girls. You may wonder why I've gathered you all here together," she said, walking over to one end of the Tower to face them. She pretended that she was holding a microphone and talking into it.

"Welcome to the Reruns!" she said. "Tonight we're showing 'The Rerun of Maeve Kaplan-Taylor's Award Ceremony'—in which Maeve finally gets it right, and thanks her friends for everything they did and are still doing to help her!"

She paused dramatically, passing out an envelope to each girl. "OPEN," she commanded in her best impersonation of an emcee's voice.

Everyone opened their envelopes. Inside were beautiful certificates, creamy white with gold trim.

THIS CERTIFICATE HONORS _____
FOR BEING AN EXTRAORDINARY FRIEND
AND HUMAN BEING AND FOR
HELPING TO MAKE THE WORLD
A BETTER PLACE!!!!

"So what I want to say," Maeve said, clearing her throat, "is thank you. Thanks for helping to make the blanket project such an amazing success. And thank you for helping me through these past few weeks and for being such great friends. And thank you for understanding even when I blew it and told you guys something that wasn't true. Most of all, thanks for being my best friends in the world!"

Everyone clapped like crazy, and the girls fought to take turns jumping up to the "pretend" microphone to give their own versions of acceptance speeches. Eventually, that turned into playing charades, and that turned into Twenty Questions, and that turned into Truth or Dare, and finally it was almost midnight and Charlotte's father was knocking on the door to the Tower, telling them that they HAD to go to sleep.

The girls opened their sleeping bags up and put them in a circle, heads facing in.

"G'night," Charlotte whispered, beginning to nod off.

"G'night," Isabel murmured.

Maeve had a sudden, overwhelming feeling of contentment. She loved being here. It felt like everything was truly okay again.

"You know what?" she said, snuggling into her sleeping bag. "You guys are the best friends on earth!"

CHAPTER
22

Apologies with Swedish Fish

Maeve was the one who came up with the plan to go to Irving's the next day.

"It's because of your Swedish Fish obsession," Katani teased her.

But everyone guessed that Maeve was really still trying to make it up to all of them.

"Come on, you guys. It's my treat today," she insisted, pulling a wad of one-dollar bills from her pocket. "I emptied my piggy bank." She giggled. "Or should I say, my GUINEA piggy bank. And I found some old money I made from baby-sitting for Sam last month." She gazed ruefully at the dollar bills. "'Course, if I'd known I had this, I would've spent it already ... But it's much better this way," she added hastily, linking arms with Katani and Charlotte. Avery and Isabel fell into step beside them, and soon the five girls were chattering away as they walked from the park toward Irving's, the tiny candy and gift store near school. The girls loved it for two reasons: the best penny candy anywhere, and the store's proprietor, Ethel Weiss.

"Ethel's kind of like the resident grandmother around here, don't you think?" Katani asked as they drew near to the store.

"Or great-grandmother," Charlotte suggested. "My mother told me that she's been here for over sixty-five years," Avery said. Ethel was a friend to almost every kid who went to Abigail Adams—as well as their younger brothers and sisters. Sometimes Maeve thought Ethel knew her almost as well as her own parents did. After all, she and Ethel went way back. Maeve had been coming to her store since she was in second grade. The girls loved everything about the store—the crowded aisles, the wonderful array of sweets and candies, and the sight of Ethel herself manning the cash register.

Today, Irving's was crowded as always. But the Beacon Street Girls made their way inside, waving hello to Ethel, who came forward to greet them with a wave and a big smile.

"Okay, girls," Ethel said, pulling up a stool and letting herself sit for a moment. "What can I get for you today? I know what THIS one wants," she added, eyes twinkling as she looked at Maeve. She reached for a bag of Swedish Fish, and Maeve giggled.

Soon everyone was finding candy, and Ethel started to ring up their purchases.

"I'm paying," Maeve said proudly, taking out her money.

Ethel looked at her quizzically.

"I owe them," Maeve said simply. "I kinda let them down about something important."

Ethel's bright eyes took in the other girls. "Candy is nice," she said simply, "but sometimes a good, old-fashioned apology is good, too, Maeve."

"She already did," Katani smiled, putting her arm around Maeve. "To be honest, I think she really just wanted to get us in here so she could get a Swedish Fish fix."

Ethel laughed. "Maeve, you always do the right thing in the end."

Several minutes later, the girls had left the store, trading candy with each other and hanging around outside the shop for a few minutes before each headed in her own direction. "Ethel's amazing," Katani said, shaking her head.

"She's not afraid to say it like it is," Avery added.

Maeve nodded. "It's like she takes care of all of us. We're all like her grandkids. I love that." She blushed again. "Even if it means getting in trouble ... again!"

"Hey, speaking of trouble," Avery said, "I just found out that I'm getting stuck being a ref for that fourth-grade soccer team I was telling you about the other day—the ones with the crazy soccer parents?"

"Ouch," Katani said. "You mean that mom who always yells no matter what call you make?"

"The very one," Avery said with a sigh. "Maybe I better go talk to Ethel again. I need some advice about diplomacy. Or a full suit of armor to protect me from those parents."

Everyone laughed.

"I'm not too worried," Charlotte said affectionately. "If anyone can stand their ground, you can, Avery Madden."

Maeve popped the last Swedish Fish into her mouth. She felt better than she had in a long, long time. Okay, she'd made some stupid mistakes lately, really stupid mistakes, but thank heavens, her family and her friends had stood by her. She had learned that when she trusted herself and listened to her own heart, she could stand up to anything.

∞

To be continued ...

Nests are so happy comfy!

Letters from the Heart

BOOK EXTRAS

Book Club Buzz

5 QUESTIONS FOR YOU AND YOUR FRIENDS TO CHAT ABOUT

1. How does Maeve react to her parents'
   decision to separate?
2. In what ways did Maeve handle the situation
   well? What mistakes did she make?
3. Who does Maeve turn to for guidance with her
   complicated family situation?
4. Who do you turn to when you need advice or
   guidance?
5. Why does Avery love the phrase "what we keep"?

The New Tower Rules
Created by the Newest Order
of the Ruby and the Sapphire

Be it resolved that *all* girls are created equal!

1. We will speak our minds, but we won't be like obnoxious or anything.
2. We won't put ourselves down, even if we aren't super-smart, super-coordinated, or a supermodel.
3. We'll be loyal to our friends and won't lie to them even if they make a mistake or do something totally embarrassing.
4. We will go for it—how will we know what we can do if we don't try?
5. We will try to eat healthy and stay active. How can you chase your dream if you can't keep up?
6. We won't just take from people and the planet. We'll try to give back good things too.

AMENDMENTS:

1. We can add as many amendments as we like.
2. We will dare to be fashion individualistas—like we're all different so why should we dress the same?
3. Sometimes we'll veg out—just because we feel like it!
4. We should have as much fun as we can.
5. We should try to save money so if we ever want to we can start a business or something someday.
6. We will try to keep an open mind about new people.

Note from Maeve
Proposed new amendment:

7. When in doubt ... phone home!

What's the vote?

Avery—this is a no brainer!
Isabel—absolutely!
Charlotte—two thumbs up!
Katani—do you even have to ask?

letters from the heart **trivialicious trivia**

1. Where is Avery's second hiding place for Marty?
   A. under her bed
   B. the laundry room
   C. the carriage house
   D. her closet

2. Name the two people, besides Maeve and Dillon, who went on the Celtics game date.
   A. Dillon's mom and Dillon's brother
   B. Dillon's sister and Maeve's brother
   C. Dillon's dad and Maeve's brother
   D. Dillon's dad and Dillon's brother

3. How did the girls get the tickets to the Red Sox game?
   A. they won a raffle
   B. they got them from Maeve's father
   C. they found them on the street
   D. they bought them at the ticket booth

4. Why did Anna and Joline chase Henry around the science lab?
   A. he stole their science project
   B. they wanted to tell him something
   C. he threw water at Anna
   D. he threw water at Joline

5. What is the name of Maeve's tutor?
   A. Matt Kierney
   B. Brendan Ryan
   C. Ruby Fields
   D. Ross Taylor

ANSWERS: 1. B. the laundry room **2. D.** Dillon's dad and Dillon's brother **3. B.** they got them from Maeve's father **4. C.** he threw water at Anna **5. A.** Matt Kierney

more *letters from the heart* Trivialicious Trivia at beaconstreetgirls.com

Don't Miss Book 4!

BEACON STREET GIRLS

A N N I E   B R Y A N T

Out of Bounds

There's a lot at stake at the seventh grade talent show.

Sneak Preview!
Out of Bounds

"So what kind of act are you going to do?" Kiki said, ignoring Anna.

"A great one," Avery said.

"Like what?" Anna challenged.

"We're going to do a magic show," Charlotte blurted out, surprising even herself.

The other BSG tried to look as if they weren't surprised.

"Right, like you know magic," Anna said.

"Charlotte studied magic in Paris," Maeve said. It wasn't exactly a lie, but it was a stretch.

"Yeah, right," Joline said.

"She did so!" said Maeve, this time with attitude.

"So, what, you're like David Copperfield or something?" asked Joline.

"More like Harry Houdini," Charlotte said. "Which reminds me, isn't it time for our vanishing act?"

Attempting an exit with attitude, Charlotte managed to send the bulletin board crashing to the floor as she turned to walk away. So much for being smooth. Katani put the board back in place and shot a glare over her shoulder, silencing the snickers from the Empress and Queens of Mean.

"Do you think Anna and Joline were born that way?"

asked Isabel when the Beacon Street Girls had finally made it down the hall.

"No way," answered Avery. "I think they practice after school to see how they can annoy everyone."

"I think they are really going to be sorry when they grow up. If they stay that way through high school, nobody is going to want to see them at our high school reunion," Maeve said vehemently.

Ready to change the subject, Avery turned to Charlotte. "So, did I hear you right? Did you just say we're going to do a magic show?"

"Sorry, it just popped out," Charlotte said.

"I think that's a great idea," Isabel said. "Avery, you should have seen the magic trick that Charlotte did the other day."

"I think it'll be fantastic," Katani said.

"I really want to do it," Charlotte said, just realizing how excited she was.

"I'm in," Maeve said.

"Me too," added Katani.

"Me three," Isabel chimed in.

"There's just one teeny problem, Charlotte," Katani realized.

"What?" the others answered in unison.

"Think about it. Charlotte is the only one who knows magic," she said just a little smugly. "What are the rest of us going to do?"

"Oh, yeah, good point," said Avery with her customary "let's get real here" attitude.

"No problem," Charlotte jumped in to reassure them all. "A magic show has lots of different parts . . . costumes, props, music. Somebody needs to get sawed in half."

"Eww!" Maeve shrilled. "Count me out."

"It's fake," Charlotte explained. "The whole thing is an illusion. That's what magic is all about. Maeve, you could be the girl in the fancy costume, who walks around the stage with funny signs. And Avery, I could make you disappear. We'll all get to do something really fun. Just wait and see."

Avery thought for a minute. "Okay, I'll do it," she said, her eyes sparkling. "But only if I get to pull Marty out of a hat." She began whooping and running down the hall.

In chorus, the Beacon Street Girls groaned and began to chase after her.

Tell your BFFs to meet you on Beacon Street!

Join the Tower Club at **BeaconStreetGirls.com** for Super-cool virtual sleepovers and parties! Personalize your locker and get $5.00 to spend on Club BSG gifts with this secret code

To get your $5 in MARTY☆MONEY (one per person) go to **www.BeaconStreetGirls.com/redeem** and follow the instructions, while supplies last.

#9 Fashion Frenzy

Katani and Maeve head to New York City to experience a teen fashion show. They learn the hard way that fashion is all about self-expression and being true to one's self.

#10 Just Kidding

Spirit Week at Abigail Adams Junior High should mean fun and excitement. But when mean emails circulate about Isabel and Kevin Connors, Spirit Week takes a turn for the worse.

#11 Ghost Town

The BSG are off to a real Montana dude ranch for a fun-filled week of skiing, snowboarding, cowboys, and celebrity twins ... plus a ghost town full of secrets.

#12 Time's Up

Katani knows she can win the business contest. But with school and friends and family taking up all her time, has she gotten in over her head?

Also . . . Our Special Adventure Series:

Charlotte in Paris

Something mysterious happens when Charlotte returns to Paris to search for her long lost cat and to visit her best Parisian friend, Sophie.

Maeve on the Red Carpet

Film camp at Maeve's own Movie House is oh-so-fabulous. But is Maeve's new friend, Madeline Von Krupcake the star of the Maddiecake commercials, really as sweet as the cakes she sells?

Freestyle with Avery

Avery Madden can't wait to go to Telluride, Colorado to visit her dad! But there's one surprise that Avery's definitely not expecting.

Katani's Jamaican Holiday

Katani's first Caribbean vacation is more mystery and adventure than lazy beach days, with a mysterious old lady, a lost heirloom necklace, and a competitive businessman scheming to take over the family banana bread bakery.